A Dollar and

A Dream

DATE DUE

JUN 1 5 2003

A Dollar and A Dream

Carl Weber
La Jill Hunt
Angel Hunter
Dwayne S. Joseph

KENSINGTON PUBLISHING CORP.
http://www.kensingtonbooks.com

DAFINA BOOKS are published by

Kensington Publishing Corp.
850 Third Avenue
New York, NY 10022

ISBN 0-7582-0755-7

First Kensington Trade Paperback Printing: October 2003
10 9 8 7 6 5 4 3 2 1

Printed in the United States of America

CONTENTS

Easy Street

Carl Weber
and
La Jill Hunt

Acknowledgments

First off I have to thank the Creator. Without Him none of this would be possible.

To Karen Thomas, my editor, my friend, and the only person in the industry I can lean on when times are hard. Thanks. Without your belief I'd be nowhere in this industry.

To Walter Zacharius, Steven Zacharius, Laurie Parkin and the entire Kensington staff, you've been better than a publishing house. You've been a second family. Drinks and dinner are on me at BEA in Chicago. Thanks for the opportunity.

To my three protegees: Angel, La Jill and Dwayne. You guys have all the talent in the world. I have no doubt that the students will someday surpass the teacher, and I will truly welcome that. Best of luck to you all.

Thanks to all the book clubs and fans who have read my books. It's you who make this whole thing worthwhile.

Last but not least, I'd like to thank all the black book stores that helped to make *Baby Momma Drama* the number one *Essence* bestseller. I may not have gotten a chance to visit each of your stores this past winter, but I'm going to try to visit every one of them in the near future.

Well, until *Player Haters* hits the stores, thanks for the ride. It's been great.

Oh, and if you get a chance, holler at your boy: *cmweb@earthlink.net*

Carl Weber

First of all I would like to thank God who has given more abundantly than I have ever deserved. I give all the honor and glory to you.

To my parents, Charles and Martha Smith, and my grandmother Minnie L. Hunt, I thank you for your undoubting faith, love and encouragement. I could never have made it this far without you.

To my husband, Corey Williams, and my beautiful daughters for your patience and presence throughout this entire process. See, dreams really can come true.

To my brother, Chaz, and my sister, Latoya (and Pie), thanks for hooking me up by baby-sitting, even when you didn't want to. I told you I had something important to do!

To Karis and Braxton and the entire Hunt, Smith, Williams, and Peck families! Thanks.

To Bishop R. L. Lewis and New Light Full Gospel Baptist Church, and Dr. K. W. Brown and the Mt. Lebanon Missionary Baptist Church. Thank God for the double portion!!!

To Yvette, you are more than a friend, you are an angel! To my friends for life—Joy, Shan, Saundra, Roxanne and Tonya. Troy, thanks for all you've done. I luv you all.

To my VZ family—there were too many to name. Robilyn, here's to the start of something great!!! Dwayne Joseph, you have the greatest listening ear and I thank you. See you on the best-seller list!!!

And last but not least to my newfound friend, advisor, confidante, and mentor—Carl Weber. Words cannot express my gratitude for taking me under your wing and guiding me along the way. You are the big brother I always wanted and never had. Through you I have learned so much and you have given more. I love you for that and will forever be indebted. And I am sure you're gonna make me pay you back, anyway!!

To anyone I forgot, I am sorry and I will catch you in *Drama Queen*.

La Jill Hunt
MsLajaka@AOL.com

1

Katrice

I barely made it into the house carrying an armload of groceries, my purse, and a handful of mail. I struggled into the kitchen and dropped the bags on the table. Clicking on the light, I saw an open forty-ounce bottle sitting on the counter, the top right next to it. He didn't even have the common sense to cover the damn thing up. Dishes were piled up in the sink and a pot of spaghetti was sitting on the stove. I just shook my head at the mess and began putting the groceries away. I stopped long enough to go through the junky living room into my bedroom and take off my uniform. I didn't bother to hang it up. *Jordan doesn't feel the need to hang his shit up. Why should I?*

I sat on my side of the bed and saw the light flashing on the answering machine. I pushed the button and listened to the messages.

"Trice, call me as soon as you get this message. I got another one of those letters from the bank, and if you can't tell, I'm pissed. Trice, you and Jordan swore you were gonna take care of this. This is not my responsibility and I am not gonna accept it. I swear—"

I clicked the delete button before my brother could finish. I knew I wasn't gonna call him. He knew it, too. It was eleven o'clock at night and I could not be bothered. Besides, what was I gonna tell him? I didn't have the money.

"Mrs. Taylor, this is Mr. Hawkins with First American Mortgage. We have been trying to get in contact with you and your brother in regard to payment on the property. It is over ninety days past due and we really need to receive payment in order to prevent foreclosure. Please give me a call at—" I cut him off, too. Lord knows I didn't wanna be bothered with him either.

I figured I wasn't gonna take a chance on receiving any more bad news, so I didn't play any more messages. I could hear someone moaning over my head and looked up at the ceiling. *Kerri must have company, and she is working it! You go, girl!* I couldn't help but smile. I didn't remember the last time Jordan wanted to get some and wasn't drunk.

I went into the bathroom and saw a wet towel in the middle of the floor. Picking it up, I put it on top of the laundry basket already piled with clothes. I picked up the heavy basket and decided that there was no better time than the present to wash clothes. I took a handful of quarters off the dresser and put the basket on a small cart, heading to the basement of the building, which served as the laundry room.

"Hey, Trice. Need some help?"

I nearly jumped out of my skin as the voice came out of the dark stairwell just as I walked out of my apartment. "Freddie! What the hell are you doing?"

"I was just waiting to catch Paul. I been waiting, but he ain't came home yet." His breath stank to high heaven and he looked like he had climbed out of the Dumpster.

"What you waiting on Paul for?" I pushed past him and dragged the cart to the basement door.

"I need for him to give me two dollars."

"You think Paul gonna give you money, Freddie?"

"He might. It's for a good cause." He smiled his yellow-stained grin and I tried not to turn up my nose.

"What? They got a sale on forties?" I smirked. He actually had the nerve to be offended.

"If they did, I'd have to stand behind your husband to get one." He laughed and left out the front door.

"At least my husband got a job, you mangy, stank-breath drunk! Get your ass off my property!" I raised my hand and Freddie took off running.

Once I was in the basement I made sure that the washer was empty and poured detergent into the machine. I pushed the quarters in and dumped the clothes. Climbing back up the steps, I gazed at the hallway walls and sighed because I knew they were in bad shape. Looking at the floors, they were even worse. It was gonna take a lot of money to fix this place up. Money I didn't have.

I walked into my apartment and headed straight for the bath. Freddie had obviously run into Paul, because I could hear them yelling.

I got into the shower and stood there at least thirty minutes. It had been a long day. Driving that damn bus is no joke. I'd been cussed out, yelled at, talked about, and spat on, and that was all in the course of one day. But the pay was all right, and I didn't get bored.

"Looks like I came home just in time," Jordan said, and pulled the curtain open.

"Jordan! Where the hell have you been? I know you got off at five. It's damn near midnight!" I yelled.

"Damn, you're sexy when you're mad." He tried to reach in but I hit him. "Is that any way to greet your husband, Trice?"

"It is when your husband left the house a goddamn wreck. Jordan, I know I cleaned this place up before I left here. You left food out on the stove and beer on the counter. This building is already raggedy as hell. What, you want us to have roaches, as well?" I snatched the curtain closed and turned the water off. I reached for my towel and went into the bedroom.

"Sounds like Kerri's getting her groove *on!* Makes me wanna do some things myself." Jordan walked behind me and ran his hands across my damp back. I must admit, it felt good, but I knew where Jordan had been and he wasn't getting no parts of this pussy tonight. I could smell the beer on his breath and it was a turnoff.

"Where have you been, Jordan?"

"I went over to the bar with Rodney," he answered.

I reached on my dresser to get the cocoa butter and began rubbing it over my body.

"Trice, you know that gets me horny when you do that. Come on, baby," he growled.

"Well, get over it. How much did you lose, Jordan?" I kept rubbing as he watched.

"Lose? What do you mean, lose?"

"Don't play stupid with me. How much did you lose gambling?"

"Who said I was gambling?"

"I said it. I know you like a book, Jordan. Now how much did you lose?"

"See. Why you gotta say it like that, Katrice? How you know I ain't win?" He took the bottle of lotion and poured some into the palm his hand. I glared at him as he rubbed his palms together.

"Because if you won, Jordan, you would have been bragging from the time you hit the door." I knew him better than he thought I did. Over the past couple of months, it had gotten worse and worse and we were getting broker and broker. I loved Jordan more than life itself. He was the best thing that ever happened to me outside of my daddy. But I was getting more and more frustrated with our current financial state, and more importantly, I was getting fed up with him

"Aw, Trice. You have no faith in your man," he said as he rubbed the lotion on my back. His hands felt so good, I began to loosen up. I let my head fall forward as he massaged my neck.

"How much, Jordan? Just tell me." I sighed.

"I was up a grand, Trice. I was on a roll. But then the dice, they got cold."

"How much?"

"Four hundred but—"

I cut him off before he could finish. "Four hundred dollars? Jordan, that's half your paycheck!" I screamed. Jordan had a decent job working for FedEx, but he gambled most of his paycheck away every week. "We barely have lights and water. Not to mention the fact that they're about to foreclose on this building!"

"What are you talking about, Katrice?"

"This building, Jordan. You know we're three months behind on the mortgage. The bank is calling every day and now they're sending Kevin letters, too. You know how hard I had to fight to keep this place. It was my daddy's dream." I could feel the tears as they filled my eyes.

"Don't worry, Trice. It will be okay. You won't lose the building. I promise, baby," he whispered.

"How can you promise something like that, Jordan? We can barely pay our own rent in this place. This is becoming a habit, Jordan, and I can't do it no more." I pulled away from him. He put his finger over his mouth and motioned for me to be quiet. Before I could cuss him out for shutting me up, he pointed to the ceiling. "I don't care who hears me," I said.

"No, listen. Kerri is yelling at somebody," he hissed. I concentrated so I could hear what he was talking about. He was right, she was yelling and she was loud. Then we heard her door slam.

"Let's go peek!" He grabbed my arm and pulled me up. We hurried into the front room and pulled back the curtain. I could see a tall man running to his Mercedes. He didn't look too happy.

"Damn. I wonder what he did?" Jordan turned and asked me.

"He probably gambled half of his paycheck away!" I huffed and got up.

"Trice, look, I told you I'm gonna take care of it. You gotta trust me. I am not gonna let you lose this place. Come on, let's go to bed."

"Where's the rest of the money, Jordan?"

"I put it in the bank," he said.

"Give me the card."

"What?"

"Gimme the ATM card." I stood up and held my hand out.

"Oh, so you don't trust me now? Is that how it is, Trice? I told you I put it in the bank."

"But I don't want it to wind up *out* of the bank. Now give me the card *and* the checkbook." I should have done this a long time ago. Jordan had lost all control and now it was time for me to gain it back.

He reluctantly reached in his brown pants pocket and pulled out a well-worn wallet. He flipped through until he found the check card for our joint account. I figured there was no point in getting his credit cards because they had been maxed out a long time ago. That done, he reached into the top of the closet and got the checkbook and thrust it at me.

"I can't believe you're doing this, Trice."

"There are a lot of things I can't believe you've done, Jordan." I looked at him solemnly. I had to ask myself if this was the same man I fell in love with three years ago.

"I'm going down to the Quick-Mart and get a beer," he grumbled.

"You got half a beer in the fridge already."

"Well, I'm going to the Quick-Mart to get some fresh air, then," he said as the door slammed behind him. I climbed in the bed and faced the wall. I had used everything I had to get this place and now I was losing all I had to keep it, including my mind and my marriage. I had to wonder if it was all worth it.

2

Paul

I could see Kerri's light was still on when I pulled up to the building. That made me pause and think, because she was usually in bed by eleven and it was way past that now. It's kinda funny how quickly I've learned her routine. I can tell you what time she gets up in the morning, what time she leaves for work, and what time she comes home without even giving it a second thought. Hell, I could probably tell you what time she takes a piss if you really wanted to know. And no, I'm not her overbearing boyfriend or some deranged stalker. I'm her neighbor, her next-door neighbor to be precise, and with the thin-ass walls in our building, I can hear everything that goes on in her apartment. And I mean everything! Especially her sex life.

The way she moans and calls out that sorry-ass old dude's name she be messin' with is enough to make a brother sick to his stomach. Don't get me wrong. I'm not trying to hate, but what the fuck does he got that I ain't got? Well, except for a Mercedes. Oh yeah, I think he's got a Lexus, too, but hell, I got a Maxima. I mean, I just don't understand why she ain't gave me none yet. I'm always nice to her. Dammit, what the fuck is she waiting for, Christmas? Shit, she don't know what she's missing. I would put it on her ass.

I closed my eyes and imagined her lying back on her canopy bed, legs spread, with her fingers pulling back the hood of her clit as I knelt down between her legs.

"Paul, oh Paul!" she'd moan as I French kiss her pooh-pooh with my catlike tongue. "Eat me, Paul. Oh God, eat me! Please, just eat me!"

Just as it's gettin' good for her, I'd stop abruptly and tease her with my words.

"Is that it, baby? Is that what you want me to do? Eat you?" She'd nod her head and I'd smile. Then I'd moisten my lips and lower my head to finish what I'd started.

"Paul! Paul! Paul!"

I shook my head and snapped myself back into reality. Shit, I wasn't in Kerri's apartment. I was still in my car and someone was out there calling my ass for real.

"Paul! Paul! Paul!"

"Who dat?" I shouted, searching the dark parking lot until a wobbly figure appeared at the rear of my car.

"It's me, Freddie. What's wrong with you? Can't you hear? I called your ass 'bout ten times. What's up, nigga, you drunk? 'Cause if you is, let me get a taste." Freddie was the neighborhood wino. A pain in the ass at times, but Freddie was generally harmless.

"Freddie, whatcha want, man?"

"I need to borrow two dollars until the day after tomorrow." He almost fell over.

"You need what?" I looked at him like he was crazy.

"I need to borrow two dollars until tomorrow. So I can play Lotto. Ain't you heard? The jackpot's fifty million."

"Yeah, I heard, but I ain't givin' you shit." I stepped out of my car.

"Come on, Paul," he whined, "with the numbers I got, I can't miss. Matter of fact, if I win I'll split it with you." He spread his hands apart as if to say, How can you beat that?

"Yeah, right." I laughed at him pityingly.

"What? Don't you trust me?"

"Hell no, I don't trust your drunk ass! Only thing I trust you to do is go down to the Quick-Mart and buy a forty so your drunk ass can get drunker."

"Damn, Paul, why you bein' so cheap? All I wanna do is buy a couple'a lottery tickets. If I wanted money for a forty, I woulda told you it was for a forty." He had the nerve to have an attitude.

"Well, why don't you get a job? Then you won't have to ask me for shit." I hit the alarm on my Maxima and headed towards my building.

"Fuck you, Paul, you cheap bastard. I should fuck up your car."

I stopped dead in my tracks and turned around. He was mumbling and probably didn't think I'd heard him, but I did.

"What'd you say?"

"Nothin'." He tried to look innocent.

"Fuck with my car if you want to, Freddie. But I'ma tell you what. If you do, you better hit that damn lottery. 'Cause after the ass-whipping I'm gonna give you, you're gonna need every dime to pay for your hospital bills. Now get away from my fucking car."

"Man, fuck you and your car," he muttered as he walked off.

Any other time I probably would've given Freddie the two dollars, but I was still pissed off about spending my money on this sister Jade I'd gone out with last night.

I'd taken her to Red Lobster and a movie, which was not my norm. Don't get me wrong. I'm not a pretty boy or anything. Shit, matter of fact some might call me a little overweight. But in a town that's got a ratio of ten women to every one man, a brother with a good job and his own place has got it made, and I was that pot of gold at the end of the rainbow. At least I was to everyone but Kerri.

I opened the main door to my building, noticing the 987 and shaking my head. We live at 5987 Easy Street, but the 5 had fallen off before I moved in and none of my fellow tenants or my landlord had found the need to fix it. Our landlord, well, she didn't fix nothin', 'cause she was in financial straits. Funny thing was that for the most part it was a fairly decent spot to live. Not located in the best neighborhood, but it was clean and the rent was cheap. The building had four apartments. Kerri and I lived in the second-floor apartments, and Rodney, this thug-ass brother I suspected of selling drugs, lived under Kerri. My landlord Katrice and her husband Jordan lived in the apartment on the bottom floor under me.

As I walked into the building Rodney was walking in also. He was probably coming home from a long day at the corner selling drugs. We exchanged pleasantries and I eyed the dude as he walked into his apartment. He acted tough, but the truth was he was soft as butter and one of these days I was gonna turn him in to the police.

I could smell the strong scent of incense coming from Kerri's apartment, which basically told me she had company. I'd been seeing her with this older dude for the past couple of months. I guess he'd spent enough so that she felt obligated to finally give the old bastard some. Lucky for him. At least somebody was getting some tonight, 'cause I sure as hell wasn't.

3

Kerri

I walked into the bathroom and the first thing I heard was some fool yelling outside my window like it was twelve in the afternoon, instead of twelve midnight. I peeked out my window and no surprise, it was Paul, yelling at poor Freddie the wino. Paul had been trying to get in my drawers ever since I moved in. Up 'til now I hadn't even given him a sniff. But as broke as I was, it might just be worth giving him some if I could get him to pay some of my back rent—so Katrice would get off my back.

Jesus Christ, what the hell was I thinking about? I couldn't believe I actually gave that shit some thought. It wasn't like I didn't already have enough male problems as it was, including the one laid up in my bed. Okay, let me stop exaggerating. Charlie wasn't that bad if you liked guys almost twice your age with receding hairlines. The only problem was he was always pushing me to get married. Then again, what should I have expected from a guy who was gonna end up paying this month's rent? You see, Charlie didn't know it, but he was more like my ATM machine than my boyfriend, and it was time for a withdrawal. Especially after I came home to find a note tacked on my door from my landlord. It read:

Kerri,
   I know times are hard but they are for everyone. You're three months behind in your rent. Pay up by Monday or you have to get out!

                                               Katrice

Well, I certainly didn't have the money to pay up but I knew who did. I'd picked up the phone and called Charlie right away.

"Hey, handsome, what time do you get off? I got something I wanna give you." I gave him my sexiest voice so he'd know what I was talking about.

"My shift ends at eleven." I could hear a lot of noise in the background, so I knew he couldn't talk long.

"I need for you to come over on your way home. What I've got for you, you've gotta have hot," I teased.

"What is it?"

"You sure are full of questions, aren't you? But if you must know, it's warm, wet, and waiting for you," I purred.

"Daaamn. I'll be there by eleven-fifteen, not a second later," he promised as he hung up the phone.

I set up the living room with candles, to set the mood. I took a bath and covered myself with the warm vanilla sugar spray I copped from Bath and Body Works. A little Luther on the stereo, my shimmering fine ass barely covered by a red satin robe, a bottle of Chianti chilling in the fridge, and by ten minutes after eleven, everything was ready.

"Hi, baby." I opened the door and greeted him before he had a chance to knock.

"Hey, yourself. So what do you have for me?" He smiled as he looked me up and down. I grabbed him by the tie and pulled him into my small living room, kissing him before I pushed him down on the sofa.

"So, how was work?"

"Work was work. Now, what you got for me?" He smiled, letting me know he knew exactly what I had for him.

"I'll tell you in a minute. Wait here. I'll be right back."

I went into the kitchen and poured him a glass of wine. Before I could turn around, I felt him behind me, reaching under my robe, caressing my ass.

"Damn, you smell good."

"I taste better," I said as I turned around and gave him a glass. He took a swallow and then kissed me full on my mouth. This was another thing I liked about Charlie. He was a take-charge kind of guy. I kissed him back and tugged at his shirt and tie until they finally came off. I was reaching for his belt when he lifted me off the floor and put me on the kitchen table. I don't know who took my robe off, me or him, but by the time I lay back, I was butt-ass naked and his face was between my legs. He licked and ate my pussy like I was a hot fudge sundae and he had just quit Weight Watchers. He moaned as he did it, and that turned me on even more. When I came, he dove in even farther.

"Mmmmm, God, this is so good," I moaned.

"Mmmmm, mmmm!" he agreed. He stopped long enough to carry me into my cramped bedroom and remove the rest of his clothes. Charlie wasn't the finest man in the world, but his cut body and big dick got me wet again.

It was me who took charge this time, laying him on his back so I could take him into my mouth. I had already decided I had to work his ass over really good because I was already three months behind on my rent and had a cutoff notice from the electric and gas company. I needed at least seven hundred dollars.

I ran my tongue along the bottom side of his penis, and then caressed his balls in my mouth. I felt his body tense up as my tongue worked its magic. I don't particularly like giving head, but with the mantra "Get the money, get the money" chanting in my head, I had a nice little rhythm going. It must have been working, because Charlie was panting and squirming, gripping the sheets. I felt him tap my shoulder, which was the signal that he was about to come. I eased my entire body on top of his and rode with the same rhythm I sucked. *Get the money, get the money.*

"Ride it, girl," he growled, and slapped my ass.

"Give it to me, then," I challenged. I leaned back slightly, rocking my pelvis into his.

"Oh God," he moaned. This got 'em every time. *Work it, Kerri. Get the money. Get the money.* I looked into his eyes and nodded.

"Come for me," I commanded. "Now!" I rocked faster and faster, driving him into a state of ecstasy. He cried out and I fell on his chest. I knew without a doubt that the money was in the bag. All I had to do was ask for it.

"God, Kerri. That shit is the bomb."

"I know." I climbed off of him and went into the bathroom to clean myself up. When I came out of the bathroom with a washcloth for him, he looked like he was knocked the fuck out. I walked back into the living room, catching a glimpse of the bills piled up on the coffee table, and remembered my plan. I climbed back into bed and lay next to Charlie's still body, wrapping my arms around him. He turned and pulled me closer to him, kissing my forehead.

"You feel so good," he mumbled.

"Only because that's how you make me feel." I snuggled closer to his warm body, deciding to make my move while he was still relaxed. "Charlie?"

"Yeah?" he answered.

"I need a favor." I began to lick his chest and nibble at his nipples.

"What is it?" he asked.

"Can I borrow some money?"

He looked down at me. "So all this was so I could give you some money, huh?"

"No! What? You think I'm some kind of 'ho? I sleep with you 'cause I care about you, not for money! I can't believe you, Charlie!" I sat up in the bed with a pout.

"No, baby. I was just playin'. I know you ain't like that. How much money you need, huh?"

"A thousand dollars for my rent." I added an extra three hundred for his last disrespectful comment.

"Damn, Kerri. What you need that much for?" He rubbed his hand between my neck and shoulders; he knew that was my spot. His lips picked up where his hands left off, and I could feel him getting hard again.

"I got to catch up on some bills, that's all. I'm behind in my rent. Can I borrow it, please?" I wanted him to answer me before we got started again. His answer would actually determine how good round two was.

"When you need it, Kerri?"

"Tonight." I could see that his round two was looking better and better.

"All right. I'll go to the ATM at the Quick-Mart and bring it back. I can get five hundred off each one of my cards," he whispered into my ear. That being said, I turned my back to him and tilted my head so he could lick the back of my shoulders. He smiled because he knew what we were about to do. Like I said, Charlie was a take-charge nigga, so no doubt doggy style was his favorite. After he hit it from the back, we took a shower and he got dressed.

"You still gonna give me the money?" I asked sheepishly.

"Yeah, gonna go get it right now."

"When you come back, are you gonna stay?" I asked as I walked him to the door.

"Nah, Boo. I got some stuff I need to take care of in the morning and I need to be on my side of town," he said as he kissed me. "Look, I'll be right back."

Although I had never actually been to his place, I knew Charlie lived clean across town. He rarely, if ever, spent the night, but I did always offer as a courtesy.

Beep, beep, beep! Something was beeping and I didn't know what the hell it was until I followed the sound and found Charlie's cell phone lying on the sofa. I reached to get it. What the fuck? Why would he care? That nigga wanted to marry me. I wondered who the hell was calling him this late at night.

"Hello?" It sounded like a question more than a greeting.

"Who is this? And where is Charlie?" an angry female shouted into my ear.

"Who the fuck is this?" It was my turn to be angry now.

"I'm his wife, bitch. Put his ass on the phone!"

"Look, ain't no Charlie here!" I screamed back at her.

"This is his cell phone, ain't it? I know his ass has been creepin', and obviously it's with you! Who is this, anyway?"

"Like I said, ain't no Charlie here!" I said, and hung up the phone. Instantly it began to ring again. I picked it up and turned it off.

Married! I couldn't believe this shit! I'd been fucking this nigga for over six months and he had a wife. Well, this shit was about to stop right now. And besides, I didn't do married men. My father cheated on my mother and it caused hell to break loose in our family. I vowed then that I would never have an affair, or be a part of an affair.

I sat on the sofa, steaming as I waited for Charlie's married ass to get back. I was gonna cuss him out from here all the way home to his rude-ass wife. I heard a car pull up and made sure it was him. I gave him time to knock and open the door.

"Man, can you believe there was a long-ass line at the Quick-Mart at this time of night? Everybody trying to buy a lottery ticket. I bought us a couple, baby." He put the tickets on the coffee table.

I didn't answer him. I just stared and looked down at his hands. There was no ring.

"Where is it?" I asked him.

"Damn, it's in my pocket."

"Not the money, you bastard. Your ring! Your fucking wedding ring!"

"Wh-wha wedding ring?" He began to stutter. "What's wrong, baby? What are you talking about?"

I handed him his phone. "Your wife called while you were gone. You fucking bastard, you're married. You were married the whole fucking time we've been together. And I thought you wanted to marry me." I was screaming as memories of my mother's pain came flooding back to me. "How you gon' disrespect me like that? How you gon' disrespect her like that? You are a trifling bastard, just like all the rest of them. Get the fuck out of my house!"

"Wait, Kerri. Let me explain." He reached for me, but I backed away before he could touch me.

"Get the fuck outta my house before I call the cops. Now!" The threat of me calling the cops must've worked, because the next thing I knew, he hauled ass and the door closed behind him. Shit, all that and I still didn't get the damn money! Just a couple of damn lottery tickets.

4

Rodney

"Goddamn it! Where the fuck is it? It's gotta be around here somewhere! I just had that shit!" I screamed, grabbing my head with both hands and pulling on the little bit of hair I had in frustration. I pulled both the cushions off my couch and threw them out of the way, desperately searching the seams of the couch and love seat for the brown envelope I'd lost. I found nothing but some loose change.

I was in trouble, big trouble, fifteen thousand dollars' worth of trouble, and the only person I had to blame was myself. If I had taken my ass over to Big Red's and dropped off the money like I was supposed to, instead of shooting craps down in the basement with that nigga Jordan, I'd be all right now. But Jordan was such a loser I couldn't resist the opportunity to take his money. Now I had eight hundred dollars of his money, but I was missing fifteen grand of Big Red's money. A position I did not wanna be in, because that shit could get me killed.

There was a knock on the door and I almost peed on myself. Could that be Big Red wondering where I was with his money? Or worse, his enforcer Bubba, the brother with no neck? God, should I open the door or should I pretend like I wasn't home? Shit, it didn't matter. If he wanted to kill me, he was gonna find me no matter what. Besides, where the fuck was I going with only eight hundred dollars in my pocket? I decided to answer the door. If it was Big Red, maybe I could reason with him.

"Who is it?" I yelled from where I was standing.

"It's Katrice."

I let out a long and thankful sigh as I walked to the door. "Hold on a sec, Trice. I'll be right there."

I didn't want her to see how trashed my apartment was, so I opened the door and stepped out in the hallway.

"Hey, Katrice, what's up?" I glanced over at the front door nervously as we talked, praying Red and Bubba wouldn't bust in the building while I was talking to my landlord.

"Look, I know you still have 'til Sunday, but I was hoping you could pay your rent a few days early so I could pay the mortgage before the first?"

"Oh shit. Didn't Jordan tell you?"

"Tell me what?"

"I'm paid up for the next two months."

"What? No, you're not," Katrice snapped. But something in her eyes said she already knew the rest of what I was about to tell her.

"Yes, I am. And I got the receipts to prove it." I went in my pocket and handed her the rent receipts Jordan had given me after I'd whipped his ass in craps. Even after that fool lost his entire paycheck to me, he still wanted to play double or nothing for my rent money.

"That motherfucker," she cursed. It looked like she was trying to hold back tears. "You beat his ass gambling, didn't you?"

"Yeah, he ain't got no luck with dice."

"Tell me something, Rodney. How much cash did you take from him?"

" 'Bout eight hundred."

She lost all expression in her face as she shook her head, mumbling, "His whole fucking paycheck. Goddamn it!"

"Hey, Katrice. You a good-looking woman. Why you fuck with that nigga anyway?"

" 'Cause I love him, Rodney. Because I love him." And on that note, she headed for the stairs, probably to talk to that fine-ass Kerri.

I watched Katrice walk up the steps, then almost shit on myself when the front door to the building flew open and Big Red walked in. He was followed by the human gorilla Bubba.

Red, a short brother who looked more like a pimp than the city's biggest drug dealer, always wore red. Today was no exception. He was wearing a red jogging suit, red sneakers, and a red baseball hat. Oh, and all his jewelry had red ruby stones.

"Where's my money, Rodney?" Red demanded coolly as he approached. "You was supposed to drop off my money six hours ago."

"I know, Red. But the funniest thing happened on my way to your office." He was in my face now and I felt like I was pinned to the wall.

"Oh yeah, what's that?"

I gave him a big, pitiful smile as I whined, "I lost the money. Ain't that funny?"

Red glanced at Bubba, then Bubba glanced back at him. They both bust out laughing and I tried to join them, though mine came out more like a nervous cackle.

"Yeah, man." Red continued to laugh. "That shit's funny as hell. Tell me if you think this shit is funny."

Before I could react, Bubba punched me in the stomach then grabbed me by the neck, lifting me off the ground like I was a rag doll.

"Where the fuck is my money, Rodney?" Big Red asked sternly. "I gave you twenty thousand dollars' worth of drugs and all I asked for was fifteen thousand dollars in return. Now I want my money or I want my product." Big Red stared at me as if he thought I was gonna answer him. But the way Bubba was holding my neck I was having a hard enough time trying to breathe. Talking wasn't even an option.

"Let him go, Bubba." Bubba did as he was told and I dropped straight to the floor like a piece of lead. Red bent over and got in my face.

"Where's my money, Rodney?" Red demanded again.

"I'm sorry, Red. I don't know how but I lost it." As much as I hated to look like a punk, I was crying by now. Red glared at me, then nodded his head three times like he'd made a decision.

"Carry this nigga in his apartment so I can put a cap in his ass," he told Bubba. Before I could even think to holler for help, Bubba's huge hand was around my neck, lifting me up in the air again. A few seconds later I was in my apartment, about ready to pee on myself. I was sure I'd be dead in ten minutes.

"Where the fuck is my money, Rodney?" Red demanded again as he pulled out a gun and pointed it at my head. He pulled back the clip and I closed my tear-filled eyes, praying that there was a heaven and God was going to accept me into it. "I asked you a question. Where the fuck is my money?"

Bubba eased up on my throat so I could speak. "I lost it, Red. I swear to God, I ain't take it. I lost it. Look around you. Can't you see I've been tearing this place apart trying to find it?"

He looked around. "Damn, this place does look like shit."

He scratched his head then reached into my pockets, pulling everything out. "Let's see what he's got, Bubba." He thumbed through the contents of my pockets. "Eight hundred dollars. Rent receipts . . ." He stuffed the eight hundred in his pocket. "Two lottery tickets. What the fuck you got these for?" He laughed and tossed them on the floor.

"A dollar and a dream," I said sheepishly, and he laughed.

"Yeah, well, you better hope your dream comes true, 'cause if you don't have my money by Monday, you gonna be dreaming permanently. Do I make myself clear?"

"Perfectly." I nodded.

"Let 'im go, Bubba."

Bubba did as he was told and I went crashing down to the floor again.

"I want my money on Monday night, Rodney. I'm not playing with you."

"I'm gonna have it, Red," I told him as he headed for the door. "I promise. I don't care if I have to rob a bank. I'm gonna have your money for you on Monday."

"You better," he growled, "or you're gonna be pushing up daisies on Tuesday."

5

Katrice

I was so pissed at Jordan. I couldn't go back into the apartment, even if he wasn't there. Just the thought of having him walk through the door and having to look into his face made me sick to my stomach. I decided to go upstairs and see if Kerri had at least part of her rent.

"You okay, Kerri?" I asked softly as I tapped on the door.

"Yeah, I'm cool," she said, and opened the door.

I followed her into the candlelit room. "Candles? And Luther? What was the occasion?"

"Happy Broke-as-Hell Night." She lifted a glass of wine in the air in an imaginary toast. She tilted it back and drank it all in one swallow. I knew she was down. Kerri hardly ever drank.

"I take it that it wasn't a happy celebration?"

"No, it wasn't. Want a glass of wine?" She stood up. "I sure need a refill myself."

"What the hell? Yeah, bring me some. Hell, bring the whole bottle," I told her.

"My girl!" she yelled as she went into the kitchen. "Where is the love of your life tonight?"

"Went to the Quick-Mart."

"What? He trying to win the big jackpot, too?"

"What jackpot?"

"Girl, you know the lottery jackpot is fifty million this week. That's why the lines have been wrapped around the building at the convenience stores. You didn't know?" She sauntered into the room carrying the bottle of wine and two glasses.

Kerri was a very attractive girl. She reminded me of one of those video chicks. Not the ghetto-fab ones, but the classy model type. She kept her long, thick hair in a ponytail piled high in the middle of her head and her face had that high-class look—almond-shaped eyes, full lips. Her body was to die for. I still didn't understand why she couldn't find and keep a good man. She was really nice, smart, and funny. Maybe there was something to her that I didn't know about.

"I didn't notice, I guess. Too much other stuff going on in my life."

"Join the club," she said, and filled our glasses.

"Look, Ker. I know your luck these past couple of months has been just as bad as mine, but I really gotta have your rent money."

"I'm trying, Trice. I damn near had it tonight, but I lost my head." She slumped back on the sofa.

"What happened up here?" I asked her out of curiosity.

"You know that older dude Charlie I been messing with?"

"Yeah. The one that said he wanted to marry you."

"Uh-huh."

"What about him?"

"Well, I decided to break him off a li'l something real good. Then I was gonna hit him up for some money for the rent."

"The way y'all were moaning and groaning, it sounded like you were breaking him in two." I laughed.

"I worked it. I know I did. Hell, he even went to the ATM to get the money for me." She sighed.

"He got you the money? Then you should be straight. Gimme my money, girl." A smile came over my face.

"I didn't finish. While he was gone—get this, girl—his mother-fuckin' wife called."

"Shut up! That nigga was married? He's been coming over here for, like, months. I thought y'all were doing a'ight." I couldn't believe it. Men are a trip. I knew I'd seen this man come over all times of the day and night. Shit, we even double-dated a couple of times. You never would've known that he was married. He sure as hell hadn't acted like it.

"Can you believe this shit?" She turned her glass up again. "And at first he tried to deny it, but then he just left when I told him I was gonna call the cops on his ass."

"So that's why you was cussing his ass out? We heard you yelling and him leaving," I told her.

"What are y'all, professional eavesdroppers or somethin'?"

"No, but when your ass is loud, and you *are* loud, we can hear everything, and I do mean everything.

"So what about the money? Did you at least get the money?"

"Hell no. I wasn't thinking. I kicked his ass out before I got the money. Now I got no man *and* no money."

"I feel for you. Men are dumb," I said, thinking about my own situation and referring to Jordan.

"Don't I know it. But I'm on a mission. I am gonna hook me a real man."

"A fine man," I added, still thinking of Jordan and his sexy chocolate self. Lord knew my husband was a loser, but he was beyond fine.

"A nice man."

"With a steady J-O-B. Don't forget he gots to have a job."

"No doubt, no doubt. And know how to romance me."

"And make sure he don't live with his mama."

"And he gotta satisfy me in more ways than one. He gotta go downtown!" Kerri stood and danced provocatively as she sang. I nearly fell off the sofa with laughter.

"And no baby mama drama!" I reminded her.

"And no wives!"

"You gotta triple-check his ass when you find him." I was almost drunk by now.

"Triple-check?"

"Credit check, criminal check, and medical check. You got to check his ass!" Tears were streaming down both of our faces and I had to pee by now. "I gotta get out of here. You got me drunk, and your ass still ain't paid your rent."

"I'll figure something out. There's a Mr. Just-For-Right-Now out there somewhere." She sighed.

"What about Rodney?" I said, thinking if I hooked them up then he could help her out and she could pay.

"Uh, I don't do criminals. I want my man to be legit. Besides, he's too small for me, and Trina from down the block said he got a little-ass dick." She winked.

"Men with little dicks have the best tongues. They make up for their shortcomings by giving us long cunnilingus." I winked back.

"Forget it. I find the thugged-out thing sexy, but it's not my style. I told you, I like my men big and legit."

"What about Paul?"

"Paul, from across the hall?" She tilted her head in thought.

"What other Paul would I be talking about?"

"I don't know, Katrice. He's nice and all, but he tries too damn hard."

"Didn't you say at one time you liked a take-charge man?" I decided to push this issue because Paul always paid his rent, and if he couldn't afford to pay it all, maybe he could afford to help Kerri pay some of her rent.

"But Paul?"

"I think you should talk to him and at least see where his head is at. Come on, Kerri, if you don't come up with this money, we're all gonna be homeless. At least try."

"So you think I should pimp myself out to Paul for my rent money, Trice? What does that say about me?" She looked at me.

"You said yourself you had thought about it at one point. Just act on those thoughts."

"No, I said I thought he was nice. I never said I wanted to fuck him," she corrected me. "Besides, he can't afford to keep me in the lifestyle I'm accustomed to."

"What lifestyle is that? Lifestyles of the broke and evicted?" I asked her and opened the door to leave. Paul was unlocking the door to his apartment across the hall.

"Oh, hi, Paul. You sure keeping some late hours," I said.

"Just taking the garbage out," he replied. "How you ladies doing?"

"Just fine. Kerri and I were just talking about you."

"For real? What about me?" He turned and looked past me at Kerri wearing the short kimono and holding her glass. I opened my eyes wide and nodded. She rolled her eyes and opened the door wider so he could get a better view.

"She asked me what type of men I liked and I told her I like my men big, like you." She licked her lips and I took this as my cue to be on my way.

"Interesting," was his only comment.

"Well, I'll check y'all later. Handle your business, Ker. Peace, Paul." I weaved past them, down the steps to my own apartment.

Jordan had not come home yet so I crawled into the bed and curled into a tight ball. I didn't know what I was going to do. Even if Kerri came up with her money, the fiasco that Jordan had worked out with Rodney still created a hole that couldn't be filled. I could see my brother Kevin now, smiling because he was right. I wasn't responsible enough to take care of this building and all that it included. I could barely pay my car note, and that was a month behind, too.

"Katrice, you don't know anything about real estate or property management. We should just sell the building, and you and Jordan can have a nice little nest egg to start off with," Kevin told me at the reading of Daddy's will.

"Daddy didn't know anything about it either, and look how much he made off of it. He had faith enough in us to leave it to us, why can't you?"

"Look, Trice, I am not trying to belittle you, or doubt you, for that matter. This is more responsibility than you can handle, and I am not gonna be the backbone for you with this one. I promise."

"I don't need you to be my backbone. That's why I have a husband. That's his job." I glared at him.

"Jordan?" He laughed in my face. "You are gonna depend on Jordan to help you do this? Trice, I just got called two days ago because the car I co-signed for you guys is past due. Now you think you can pay the mortgage on a building?"

"The car note has been taken care of. There was a bank error, but now it's corrected." I didn't tell him that the error had been that Jordan told me he put five hundred dollars in the checking account when he only put in two-seventy-five.

"Fine, Trice. You do your thing. But I am not gonna be responsible for whatever happens. I mean that."

"Whatever, Kevin. I know what I'm doing."

He was right. I wasn't responsible enough, and Jordan sure as hell wasn't no kind of backbone. The door squealed open as he tried to sneak in. He crept in the room and I could hear the jingling of his belt as he removed his pants. He went into the bathroom and brushed his teeth and gargled. Then, carefully, oh so carefully, he eased into bed. When he saw that I didn't move, he snuggled against me and put his arm around my body like he did every night. I chose not to say anything because I was sleepy from the wine, exhaustion, and depression all rolled into one. I fell asleep with the building on my mind, my daddy in my heart, and tears on my pillow.

6

Paul

"So, Kerri, maybe we can have dinner sometime?" I wasn't sure, but it looked like Katrice was giving me a hint to try and get with Kerri before she left. So I was gonna see where it went. "How about Red Lobster?"

"I don't do Red Lobster, but you can take me to Legal Seafoods if you want."

"Ah, I don't know much about Legal Seafoods. What's it like?"

"It's expensive, Paul. Like me." She smiled and it seemed like the entire hallway lit up. "Do you think you can afford a woman like me? A high maintenance woman?"

"Well, yeah, I think so. I mean, I like you, Kerri. I'd do whatever it takes to keep you happy."

"Really? Well, I might keep you to that," she teased. "Look, I have to check my calendar and I'll get back to you about dinner, okay?"

"Yeah, sure, no problem. Let me know when you check your calendar." I frowned. She was giving me the runaround just like usual. Damn, I shouldn't have even asked her out. I picked up my trash and took a step towards the stairs.

"Hey, Paul," she called. I stopped and turned around. "I'm having a couple of people over the day after this Saturday night to watch the Tyson fight. Why don't you bring over a bottle of Dom Perignon and a bottle of Moet, say around nine? You can be my date."

"Sure, but why you gonna need both?"

"Because I'm not quite sure what I'm gonna be thirsty for. I thought you said you'd do whatever it takes to make me happy?"

"I did."

"Then I'll expect you to have both. Now I've gotta get some sleep." She leaned over and kissed my cheek. My dick got hard right away. Thank God she didn't look down at my sweatpants before she closed the door, because my shit was poking out so far my pants looked like a tent.

I picked up my bag of garbage and walked down the stairs with a stupid grin on my face. I never really thought I'd have a shot with Kerri. I guess I always thought she was too high maintenance for me. And in truth, she still might be. Dom *and* Moet? But I wasn't about to let a chance like this go by without trying. Kerri had to be one of the finest women I'd ever met.

When I got downstairs I went around to the side of building where the trash cans were. Freddie was there, rummaging headfirst through one of the cans. It turned my stomach to see a grown man with his hands all up in that nasty shit.

"Freddie, what the hell are you doing, man?"

"I'm trying to find this brown envelope for Rodney. He said he was gonna give me two dollars if I found it. I'm gonna buy me some lottery tickets." He bent back over into the can and started digging again. I grabbed him by his coat and pulled him out.

"Freddie, man, get the hell outta there. Here, I'll give you the two dollars." I reached in my sweatpants pocket, pulled out two dollars, and handed it to him.

"Thank you, Paul. Thank you!" He looked like he was gonna bust a gasket. "Man, when we hit, I'm gonna split it with you. I swear to God."

"A'ight, Freddie, you do that. Just don't be going through no more garbage. You hear?"

"A'ight, Paul. No problem. Look, I'm gonna go get in line so I can buy our tickets." He turned around and headed straight for the Quick-Mart, which meant he'd be guzzling down a forty-ounce in about ten minutes.

I put my trash in the can and covered it with the lid. When I turned to go back inside, Rodney was standing in my way. I couldn't stand his ass. Poisoning our people with his drugs and shit.

"Where's Freddie?" he growled.

"I gave him two dollars and sent him on his way. Why the fuck you have him going through the trash?"

"That's none of your damn business. Ain't nobody tell you to send Freddie nowhere." He took a step toward me, trying to get all up close and personal. Only problem was, he was about six inches shorter than I was and put no fear in my heart.

I pushed him backwards. "You better get the fuck out my face, man."

What?" He threw his hands in the air, rocking his head like he was about to do something. "You talking to me, nigga? You better recognize."

"Recognize what? That you a thug?"

"You looking to get fucked up, ain't you?"

"If you feel froggy? Leap. Just make sure you don't get stomped in the process. 'Cause you don't scare me." We stared at each other, eye to eye. I was not about to back down to this sorry-ass fool, and he sure as hell wasn't really gonna step to me. Rodney was a punk when it came right down to it.

"You lucky I got some shit to take care of, otherwise *CSI* would be looking for a body bag for your ass." He tried to sound menacing, but it wasn't working on me.

"Let them know I'm a size forty-two," I told him.

7

Kerri

I'd just stepped out of my apartment and headed downstairs to pick up a few things for my party tomorrow night when I ran into Paul coming up the stairs. I gave him the once-over, and I had to admit, in a suit and tie he looked much more respectable than I thought.

"Hey, Paul." I smiled. "Don't forget the party. Oh, and I checked my calendar. I'm free for dinner on Saturday." He started to grin from ear to ear but then his smile disappeared.

"Kerri, do you think we could do it next weekend?"

"Next week? Why, you got something to do?"

"Well, actually no, but I had them fax over the menu from this Legal Seafoods place to my job, and well, it's kind of expensive. I'm gonna be a little short on funds till payday next week."

"Damn, you trying to tell me buying dinner is gonna break you like that?" I was starting to think Katrice was wrong. His broke ass was not for me.

"No, not normally, but Katrice asked me to help her out and pay my rent a little early. None of us wanna see her lose the building." He was right, but that was beside the point.

"Paul, I'm not gonna lie to you. I don't deal with disappointment very well. I was really looking forward to going out with you this weekend and sharing a little one-on-one time in my apartment after dinner, if you know what I mean." I winked at him and he swallowed hard, looking like he was going to melt. I continued to walk down the stairs with a wide smile. When I got finished with him, he'd come through even if it meant pawning everything in his apartment.

I got to the front of the building and Freddie was sitting on the step drinking a forty-ounce like there was no such thing as an open container law in our town.

"Freddie, what are you doing? You know you're not supposed to be drinking out here. If Katrice catches you, she's gonna skin you alive."

"Well, I guess I better finish this off so I don't get caught," he slurred. "Cheers, Kerri."

He lifted the bottle in a salute to me then tipped it toward his lips. He finished most of what was left in one long, impressive gulp, then burped loudly, straightening up his back.

"Excusssssssse me!"

"Damn, Freddie, that's nasty!"

He grinned and I had to let out a laugh. That Freddie sure was a character.

I looked down the block to my left, then to my right. "Damn, I could have sworn I parked it right there. Where the hell is it?"

"Something wrong, Kerri?" Freddie asked from his seat on the step.

"I could have sworn I parked my car across the street."

"You mean the red Honda Civic that was parked over there?"

"Yeah, that's my car. Where is it?"

"It's gone."

"It's gone? Gone where? What happened to my car, Freddie?" My eyes were as wide as silver dollars.

Freddie shrugged his shoulders. "I don't know where they took it. But they took it."

"They, who? Who took my car, Freddie?"

"The cops took it. Or was it the sheriff?" He scratched his head, looking confused. "I'm not really sure, but it had something to do with tickets. They said you owed a lot of tickets. That's why they towed you."

"They towed my car for tickets." I felt like I was gonna faint and the tears just started rolling down my face.

"You a'ight, Kerri?"

"No, Freddie, I'm not all right."

"Freddie! What the hell are you doing on my stoop with that bottle?" I looked up. Katrice was getting out of her car and she looked hot. Freddie, obviously not a stupid man, jumped up and was running wobbly down the block. Katrice followed him a few steps then stopped, turning back toward the building.

"Kerri, you seen that fool drinking on my stoop. Why didn't you stop him?" I didn't answer her and she walked up closer. "Did you hear me, Kerri?" When she got close enough she said, "What's the matter? Why you crying? What happened, Kerri?"

"They towed away my car, Katrice."

"Oh Lord. When it rains it pours, doesn't it? I just found out they're gonna sell this building on Sunday if I don't come up with ten thousand dollars."

My problems seemed miniscule compared to hers. "I'm sorry, Katrice."

"It's all right. I'll make a way. How much do you owe in tickets?"

"I don't know. Probably about seven hundred dollars."

"I told you about parking wherever the hell you please. You can't flirt your way out of tickets if you're not there when they write them, Kerri."

"I know. I was gonna pay them next week." Katrice gave me this skeptical look like she knew I was lying.

"Come on in the house so I can get out of this uniform and I'll make you a cup of tea." Katrice and I drank tea with brandy in it for almost forty-five minutes before Jordan came in the house.

"What time is it?" he demanded.

"Almost ten o'clock. Why?"

" 'Cause they're getting ready to give the lottery results." Jordan ran in front of the TV and turned it on.

"You buy any tickets, Kerri?" Jordan asked as Katrice and I walked over to the sofa.

"Just the ones that sorry-ass Charlie left when I found out he was married."

"Would it be funny or what if he left you the winning ticket?" Katrice laughed.

"No, it wouldn't be funny," Jordan added, " 'cause that would mean my tickets aren't the winner."

"Kerri, run get your tickets so we can see if you won."

I knew it was a long shot, but I ran upstairs to grab the handful of tickets. I was glad I didn't burn them like I started to. I made it back down to her apartment just in time to see the blond woman with the plastic smile announce it was time. Katrice had her own line of tickets spread on the table in front of her and so did Jordan. He looked like he must have spent two or three hundred bucks. I arranged mine on my lap.

"And the first number is nineteen," Blondie said as the plastic ball with the one and nine filled the television screen. I looked down at my tickets and scanned for the number. All of a sudden, I saw it. It was right on the next to the last ticket.

"I got that," I said.

"Me, too." Jordan smirked.

"Not me," Katrice mumbled.

"The next number is twenty-six."

I scanned the ticket and saw that I had it on two tickets, including the one that held nineteen.

"I got that, too." I frowned at the ticket and picked it up to be sure. Maybe my luck was changing.

"I ain't got that shit on any of these," Jordan snapped.

"Fifty-four."

My heart began to beat so fast, I was squirming in my seat.

"Girl, you got that?" Trice looked at me. I couldn't answer her. I just nodded.

"Oh shit," Jordan yelled. "If you hit, you gonna split it with us. Right, Kerri?" I didn't answer him. I just waited for the next number.

"Fourteen."

I glanced at the ticket and started screaming, "Yes! Yes! Yes!"

"That's four, Kerri. You can do it," Katrice encouraged.

"Kerri, you gonna split it with us if you win?" Jordan asked again, and again I ignored him.

"Thirty-three."

I looked at the ticket, hoping thirty-three was there, but it wasn't.

"Damn." I sighed.

"Don't worry. If you get at least five numbers, you still get a couple grand," Katrice told me, still excited.

"And the final number is . . . nine! If your ticket has the following numbers, nineteen, twenty-six, fifty-four, fourteen, thirty-three, and nine, you are the winner of the fifty-million-dollar jackpot." She smiled her plastic smile.

"Did you get five out of the six?" Trice asked.

"Yeah, I did." I nodded.

"You did?" Jordan's eyes got huge.

"I got all six. Problem is, they're on three different tickets. Four numbers on one, two on the other, and one by itself." I was frustrated and balled the tickets up in a tight ball.

"Well, I guess I'm gonna lose this building. Thanks to my husband gambling up the rent money."

"Don't fucking start, Katrice," Jordan cursed.

"I wouldn't have to start if you didn't fuck up my money, Jordan!" She rolled her eyes, almost daring him to reply.

Jordan didn't say another word. He just grabbed his coat and walked out. Katrice sat back and folded her arms. She looked like she wanted to cry. Hell, if she did, I'd probably join her. But I knew she wasn't in the mood for company anymore, and I really didn't want to be there either.

"Girl, I'm gone," I told her, and turned to leave.

"Where you going?" she murmured.

"Upstairs to bed. Maybe my life will be better in my dreams." I walked out and closed the door behind me before she could say anything more. I was so fucking depressed that I didn't see Rodney coming out of his place and bumped right into him.

"I take it you ain't win, either." I pointed at the small slips of paper in his hand.

"Fuck, naw. I ain't win shit. And you need to watch where the fuck you going." He glared at me. I really didn't know Rodney all that well, but I did know that he and Paul had some words on more than one occasion. I tried to stay clear of him, but I wasn't going to be disrespected either.

"Whatever. You bumped into me, remember?" I turned to go up the steps and I heard him mumbling something.

"What did you say? I know you ain't say nothing about me," I said.

"I said shit around here 'bout to get real crazy and you mother-fuckers better watch the fuck out. I'm getting tired of everyone around here's mouth. And I better not find out any of y'all got that envelope."

"What is that supposed to mean?"

"It means exactly what I said." He looked at me like I'd stolen something. I didn't know what he was talking about and didn't want to know.

I just looked him in his eyes and said, "You better not do noth-ing stupid."

He pushed the door so hard that it hit the other side of the build-ing. I shook my head. That's why I don't do thugs. They're more moody than a woman on her period.

I didn't even bother taking off my clothes when I got in my apartment. I just climbed in my bed and tried to sleep my bad luck away.

8

Paul

I walked into Joe's Liquor Store next to the Quick-Mart about quarter to nine, wearing a suit I just got out of the cleaners and carrying a dozen roses. I was about to head over to Kerri's little get-together, but before I showed up I had to pick up the champagne she requested.

"What's up, Paul?" The owner smiled at me as if he was impressed. "Got a hot date?"

"I don't know how hot it is, but I'm hoping to get lucky. Let me have a bottle of Dom Perignon and a bottle of Moet."

"Wow, you goin' all out, aren't you? New suit, a dozen roses, a bottle of Dom Perignon and a bottle of Moet. Damn, who's the lucky lady?"

"You know Kerri from my building?"

"You mean fine-ass Kerri? The one with the shape that looks like an old-fashioned Coke bottle?"

"Yeah, that's Kerri all right." I smiled with pride.

"You going out with her? How the hell did you pull that off? No offense, Paul, but isn't she outta your league?"

"I thought so, too," I told him, "but when they call you up from the minors, you don't say no. You take your ass up there and try to act like the big dogs. Hopefully you'll impress somebody enough that they'll keep you around."

"Well, I hope she keeps you around, Paul, 'cause I can't think of a guy who deserves it more than you."

"If everything works out the way I plan, I'll be around every night from now on."

"You go, boy. Hit that shit one time for me." He laughed and I joined in. "Man, let me get your champagne out the fridge so you can be with that fine-ass woman."

Joe walked the short distance to the refrigerator and pulled out two bottles. He placed them on the counter then stepped over to his register.

"You need a corkscrew with that, Paul?"

"No, if she doesn't have one, I'm sure I've got one at the house."

"All right. That'll be one hundred sixty-seven twenty-eight."

"A hundred and sixty-seven dollars?" I snapped back at him. "That's gotta be wrong."

He glanced at the register. "Nope, it's right."

"Are you crazy? I could take five women out for that."

"Look, you were the one who said you wanted to hang with the big dogs. Big dog champagne costs seventy dollars a bottle and up."

"Are you serious?"

"Yep."

"Well, what are the little dogs drinking these days?"

"I've got some Andre's over here for ten-ninety-nine. It may give you a hangover, but it's champagne, and champagne's champagne, if you ask me."

"Okay, then let me have six bottles of the Andre's and we'll see if we can make up for quality with quantity."

"That sounds good to me, but are you sure Miss Thing is gonna go for this?"

"Don't worry about Kerri. I got something for her."

Ten minutes later I was standing in front of Kerri's door with a dozen roses in one arm and the champagne in the other. She was playing some nice jazz and I could hear people through the door in the background, most notably that loud-ass Jordan.

I knocked on the door and Kerri answered, wearing a black strapless evening gown that showed off every curve of her hour-glass figure.

"Hey, Paul." She smiled seductively and kissed me on the cheek.

"Hi. Sorry I'm late."

"Oh, don't worry about that. The fight doesn't start for a good half hour."

"These are for you." I handed her the flowers.

"Oh, Paul, they're lovely. Come on in." She took hold of my arm and I walked into her apartment. "Everybody, Paul's here and he's brought champagne."

The crowd turned and everybody but Rodney smiled. Kerri placed the flowers in a vase, then turned to me. "Let me have the champagne, Paul, so I can put it on ice."

"Sure." I handed her the bag.

"Wow, this is heavy. You must have gotten more that two bottles." She reached into the bag.

"Yeah, I got six, but I didn't get—" I didn't have to finish my statement. Her eyes finished it for me.

"What the fuck is this? This isn't Dom or Moet," she yelled. Everyone in the room turned toward me, and to say I was embarrassed was an understatement.

"Yeah, I know. That stuff was eighty dollars a bottle. Why pay that much for something you're gonna drink in half an hour? I could be loaning that money to Katrice so she won't lose the building."

I smiled at Katrice, hoping she might come to my rescue, but after she glanced at Kerri she never said a word. Kerri's face said it all. She was not a happy camper. Thank God Jordan put in his two cents.

"I don't give a damn how much it costs. Does it have alcohol in it?" Jordan asked.

"Yeah," I replied.

"So what's the problem? Crack them babies open. We're not on Park Avenue. More like Broke Avenue up in here." He took the bottle out of Kerri's hand and it seemed like the party went back to normal, though Kerri basically ignored me for most of it.

About midnight, the crowd thinned down to the people who lived in the building. That's when Kerri, who'd been pouting all night, finally approached me.

"Can I speak to you for a minute?"

"Sure, what's on your mind?"

She pulled me over into a corner. "I looked at my calendar again and I'm busy this weekend."

"Okay. What about next weekend?"

"I'm pretty much busy from now on where you're concerned, Paul. I can't fuck with you. You're too cheap for me."

"Why, Kerri? Just because of the champagne? Because nobody cared. They drank every last drop outta all six bottles."

"I care, Paul. I told you what I wanted and you couldn't live up to those standards."

"Come on, Kerri. Give me a chance. Let me make it up to you," I pleaded.

"I already gave you a chance, Paul, and you blew it." She walked away and Jordan walked up behind me. He handed me a glass of champagne.

"Man, fuck that chick." He waved his hand at Kerri's back.

"I'm gonna do just that, Jordan my man. Just you wait and see. She don't know it, but soon enough Miss Kerri's gonna be begging me to give her some."

"What? You plan on dying and coming back as Denzel Washington or something? 'Cause that chick's all about the money." He finished off what was left of his champagne. "So did you hear the news?"

"What news? My mind has been on nothing but Kerri the last day or two."

"You ain't hear? Whoever hit the lotto bought their ticket over at the Quick-Mart across the street. Somebody from around here is walking around with fifty million dollars in their pocket."

"No shit. Get the fuck outta here."

"For real."

I reached in my pocket and pulled out five lottery tickets as casually as I could. "Damn, I ain't even check my numbers yet."

"Man, what the fuck you waiting for?" Jordan seemed more excited than I did. "Hey, Kerri," Jordan shouted. "You got today's newspaper?"

"Look on the kitchen counter," she shouted back.

Jordan and I walked over to the kitchen counter and I flipped through the paper until we found the page with lottery results.

The first two tickets didn't even come close. But the third ticket made me look at Jordan and say, "Look at this ticket and tell me if I'm seeing what I think I'm seeing."

Jordan looked down at the paper, then at the ticket, and did a triple take. Then he looked up at me with this astonished, glassy-eyed look.

"Nigga, you just won the motherfuckin' lottery!"

All I could do was smile. I stood frozen and speechless, staring at the ticket. Jordan was jumping up and down, screaming his head off like he'd just won instead of me.

"Paul just won the lottery! Paul just won the motherfuckin' lottery, y'all!"

By the time he finished screaming, everyone in the room had surrounded me.

"Stop lying. He ain't hit that shit," Rodney snapped.

"Yeah, he did. Show him the ticket, Paul."

I handed Rodney the ticket and he checked it against the newspaper.

Rodney looked up with the same astonished look that Jordan had when he first realized I'd won. "Goddamn, this motherfucker really did hit the lottery," Rodney exclaimed.

Everyone was congratulating me and shaking my hand. Everyone but Rodney, that is. He was still holding my ticket like it was his.

"Hey, Rodney." I stuck my hand out.

"What?" Rodney looked like I snapped him out of some serious daydream.

"Can I have my ticket back, please?"

He looked around at all the people staring at him, and then sighed as he handed it over.

9

Kerri

I looked at the clock and decided it was time to make my move. I took a quick shower and made sure I smelled good in all the right places. I applied some gloss to my lips and then slipped on the kimono that Paul was checking me out in the other night. I still couldn't believe he'd won the lottery. After doing a quick mirror check, I eased my door open and crept across the hall. I gently tapped on the door and posed in the hallway. It took him a few a seconds to answer the door.

"Kerri? What's up?" he asked.

"Nothing. I couldn't sleep so I decided to see what you were up to. You weren't busy, were you?" I asked him innocently.

"No, I was about to watch a movie I rented."

"Can I watch it with you? I can't sleep."

"Sure."

I walked into the dim apartment. I knew all of the units had the same layout and size, but for some reason Paul's seemed much bigger. His living room held a black African-print sectional with a coffee table shaped like a panther. The walls were covered with masks and African artwork. The brother had taste. There was a mahogany entertainment center holding a big-screen TV and a stereo, and instead of lamps, he had what looked like lanterns burning candles instead of lightbulbs. I was impressed. Maybe I should have got with this brother a long time ago.

"This is nice. I like it," I told him.

"Thanks. I'm glad you do. I didn't think it would impress someone as high maintenance as yourself. I know how you hate to be disappointed." He smiled smugly.

"Touché. Look, I'm sorry about everything I said earlier. I'm just used to getting my way." I sat on the sofa and rubbed my hand across the sleek material. "So, what movie were you about to watch?"

"*Red Dragon*." He sat near me, but not too close.

"Oooh, scary. I wouldn't dare watch that by myself," I said. "I get afraid of the dark."

"Don't worry. I'll protect you from the bogey man."

"I'm sure I'll be safe with someone like you around."

He picked up the remote and hit *Play* on the DVD player. I eased closer to him and put my hand on his leg. He didn't move. I knew he was playing hard to get but I was about to play even harder. I had one goal and one goal only: *get the money!* I also had the advantage in knowing how bad he wanted to get with me. There was no way he was gonna miss out on an opportunity like this, and neither was I.

"Have you seen this?" I looked up at him and let my hand linger on his thigh.

"Yeah, I rented it a couple of times," he answered and let his arm touch my shoulder.

"Is it good?" I touched him a little more firmly.

"That's why I keep renting it. You always return for more if it's good. That's true about everything in this world." He was no longer looking at the TV, but at me.

"Is that true when it comes to you?"

"I've had no complaints. Women always seem to come back for more." He began to finger my earlobe. The light from the TV cast a sensual aura in the room. For some reason I was getting turned on, and I wasn't sure if it was the fact that he was gonna get all that money or if it was just him.

"So you think if you hit it once you can hit it twice, huh?"

"I got the magic stick! I know if I hit once, I can hit twice."

"Okay, fifty cents. You talk a good game, but it's results that matter." I positioned myself so that he could see my breasts through the thin robe. He responded exactly the way I wanted him to. I could feel him getting harder as I rubbed his crotch. *Get him, girl. Get him.*

"Yeah, well. I got skills to back it up." He tugged at my belt and let my robe open. I raised myself up and straddled his lap. I had my moves planned carefully as I looked into his eyes.

"Prove it," I whispered into his ear, and licked his lobe. I could feel his fingers running across my breasts and my nipples hardened. He kissed along my collarbone and leaned me back slightly. I thought I was about to fall and I reached to brace myself.

"I got you. Chill," he said, and smiled as he cupped my breast with one hand and braced my back with the other. I put my hands around his head and shivered as he gently sucked one nipple, then the other. I arched my back and a moan escaped from the back of my throat. I looked down and saw him looking up at me, smiling. "See. And I'm just getting started."

Wait a minute, Ker, you're supposed to be the seducer here, not the one being seduced. I regained control of the situation and remembered the game plan. I put my hands on his ears and tilted his head toward me. I kissed him with such fullness that it seemed like our mouths were made for each other. I slid out of my robe and his hands began to stroke my back. I was dripping by this time, which surprised me. Not a lot of guys were able to get me this wet this quickly. I knew that if his bedroom skills were anything like the foreplay, I was gonna have to pull out all the tricks. But as desperate as I was, I wouldn't care if he wanted to tie me up to the bedpost and flick sunflower seeds at me. I was down for whatever.

"Let's go to your room," I said and stood up.

He took my hand and led me down the hallway. His bedroom was just as nice as the living room. It had a jungle motif with zebras, tigers, leopards, and such. He had a huge four-poster bed in the middle of the floor. I turned around and faced him as I climbed in. I sat right in the middle and wiggled my finger at him. "Come here."

"No, you are gonna come here." His arrogance turned me on even more. He stripped his clothes off and my eyes widened at the size of his manhood. The brother was hung, and somehow I knew I was not gonna be left short. Goddamn, I was turned on. *Get the money, get the money, don't forget to get the money.*

He climbed onto the bed, and before he could do anything, I was sucking on him like a super-sized bomb pop. He began to groan and tell me how good it felt. *So he's a talker,* I thought. I decided to spice things up and see if he was kinky. I stopped what I was doing and crawled in his face.

"Paul, where's the ticket?"

"Huh?"

"I wanna touch it. I want to rub it on my breasts while you're doing me."

"Don't play, Kerri. You're blowing my high," he sat up and told me.

"Come on, Paul. Let me see it," I begged. He reached in his nightstand and handed me the ticket. I looked at the numbers and smiled.

"Don't smile at that bullshit. I got something to really make you smile." He pushed my legs damn near over my head and thrust his dick in, causing me to scream. He was grinding and stroking me like an expert. I was loving every minute of it. And I held the ticket over my chest as he took me on the ride of my life. I couldn't believe that I was getting dick this good. And to think I could have been getting this shit every night if I had just looked past the money. But now it didn't matter, 'cause it was a fifty-million-dollar dick and I had the ticket in my hand to prove it. *I got the money, I got the money, I got the money!*

"Paul, oh Paul. That's it, baby. Tear that shit up! Tear it up! Please, baby, don't stop. I love you, Paul. I love you. I'm not lying, Paul, I'm in love with you." All of the tension I had been building up over the past days released as we both came together.

"Ahhhhhhh!" he moaned as he collapsed on my chest. We were both covered in sweat and breathing like we had just finished a two-hour Tae-Bo class.

"That was . . . that was the best I've ever had," I huffed honestly when I was finally able to talk.

"So what do you think? Can I hit it again or what?" He smiled.

"You can hit it anytime you want." I chuckled.

"Good. So what'd you do with that ticket?" He began looking around the bed.

"It's right there." I pointed at his chest, where the ticket was sticking to him like a tattoo. I peeled it off his chest then handed it to him. Then I lay on his chest until I fell asleep.

I don't know what time it was when I woke up, but it was time to seal the deal. I wasn't about to let Paul go, but I also wasn't about to forget all my bills and my car, which I needed to retrieve from impound. "Paul." I shook him until he was fully awake.

"What?" He smiled as he rolled over. "You want some more?"

"Yeah, actually I do, but before we get started, can I ask you something?"

"Sure, what's up?" He started to kiss his way downtown. I hesitated, enjoying his kisses until he hit my spot.

"Oh God, does that feel good," I moaned.

"Don't worry about what I'm doing. Ask your question."

"I'm trying, but it's hard to concentrate with you licking me like that."

"Okay, I'll stop." He lifted his head and that made me mad.

"No, don't stop," I shouted.

He lowered his head and continued to lick me like I've never been licked before. After I came a good five or six times, he smiled confidently, kissing his way back up to my face. He kissed me passionately, then rolled me over and mounted me from the back. Goddamn, that shit was even better than what he did last night. And to be honest, I'd completely forgotten about the money. I was concentrating solely on the dick. He was hitting that shit so good the bed was moving across the room, and I didn't give a damn if it went right through the wall as long as he didn't stop. When he came, I came with him, and I'm sure everyone in the building knew it by the way he was making me scream.

"Didn't you say you wanted to ask me something?" He rolled off me and I slid up his chest so we were eye to eye.

"Uh-huh," I huffed.

"Well, what is it?"

I was so spent I was tempted to just say, "Forget it. I'll talk to you about it later," but I had promised myself I wouldn't forget the money and this was an opportunity to get it.

"Now that you have all this money, do you think you could give me a loan? I mean, with fifty million, you won't even miss a hundred thousand or two, would you?"

He laughed halfheartedly. "Did you just ask me to loan you a hundred thousand dollars?"

"Paul, if you gonna be my man, I need you to help me get back on my feet." I reached down and took hold of his dick. To my surprise, it was soft as cotton. I didn't understand that, because it was just hard a second ago.

"So all this was about was the money?" He sat up and damn near pushed me off him.

"No, I like making love to you. Hell, I love making love to you.

I'm just saying now that you got the money, you need to help a sister out. You wanna help me out, don't you?"

"Yeah, Kerri, I can help you," he said gently, making me smile. "I can help you get the fuck out of my apartment, that's what I can do! I should've known you were a gold-diggin' 'ho when you started talking that Legal Seafoods and Moet bullshit. But for some reason I thought you were really digging me for me. Just get the fuck out."

"Paul, it ain't even like that and you know it."

"All I know is that you ain't no different than any other 'ho on the street, except they ask for their payment up front."

"Paul, you've got this all wrong."

"No, I don't. You're a gold-digger, Kerri. You don't care about me. All you care about is money. The funny thing is, a woman doesn't have to ask a real man for money. He makes sure his woman is taken care of no matter what. Now get the fuck out of my apartment." He pointed at the door.

"You gonna regret this, Paul."

"I already do, Kerri. Believe me. I already do."

With that being said, I gathered my dignity and myself and sauntered back across the hall to my own apartment. *I still ain't get the money!*

10

Rodney

I left Kerri's apartment with a nice buzz and headed down the stairs after the get-together she had. I still couldn't believe that punk Paul hit the lottery! But I'd seen the ticket with my own eyes, so there wasn't no denying that. I guess that's just the way shit is. All I needed was fifteen thousand to make me happy and that motherfucker upstairs was sitting on top of fifty million. I was gonna have to talk to him tomorrow and see if he could hit me off with a loan, otherwise I was gonna have to get out of town.

I walked into my apartment and flipped on the light. I almost jumped out of my skin when I saw big-ass Bubba sitting in my recliner.

"Jesus Christ! What the fuck are you doing here? I thought I had 'til Monday night to pay y'all. How'd you get into my apartment, anyway?"

Bubba got up out of the recliner and walked over to me. "You do have till Monday," Bubba growled. "But Big Red wanted me to make sure you understand how serious we are about our money. We wouldn't want you to leave town or anything like that."

"I wouldn't leave town," I told him nervously.

"Oh yeah, so why the hell are your bags packed in your bedroom?"

"Ah, ah . . ."

He grabbed me by the neck and lifted me off the ground, giving me one hard smack across the face. Blood sprayed from my nose.

"Big Red wanted me to ask you a question. Do you know anybody who lives at 365 Chestnut Road?"

"Yeah, my mom. Why?" *Oh shit. Not my family!*

"What about 78 Wilkens Street?"

"My baby's mom and my son. Why? What you want with them?" I was trying to sound tough, but I was so scared I was about to piss on myself.

" 'Cause if you're not here on Monday, we gonna see them. And believe me, it's not gonna be pretty. Understand?" He dropped me on the floor and inspected his shirt. "You got blood on my shirt. Add seven dollars to that fifteen thousand, 'cause you gonna pay for it to be cleaned."

Bubba walked out of my apartment and I lay on the floor for a few minutes, trying to think of my next move. I knew Bubba wasn't joking about going to see my mom or my baby's mom if I wasn't here on Monday. I got my ass up, went over to the phone, and dialed my mother's number.

"Hello?"

"Ma, it's me, Rodney."

"Rodney? Do you know what time it is?"

"Yeah, Ma. It's about one o'clock."

"One o'clock? Why are you calling me at one o'clock in the morning? You not in jail, are you? 'Cause I ain't got no bail money. You hear me?"

"No, Ma. I'm not in jail. I just called to tell you I love you."

"Ah, baby, I'm sorry. Mama loves you, too."

" 'Night, Ma."

" 'Night, Rodney."

I hung up the phone and stared into space. Originally I was gonna ask her to go down South for a few weeks until I could get things straight with Big Red. But once I heard her voice I knew she wouldn't have listened to me. And my baby's mama, knowing her, she would be even more stubborn. So I was stuck. Skipping town was out of the question now.

I looked up at the ceiling. Paul had somebody up there and he was getting his groove on. I sat and listened for a while, then I fell asleep.

When I woke up I could hear Paul going at it again. I'm not sure who he was with, but whoever she was, he was putting it on her. It sounded like his bed was going from one end of the room to the other.

11

Katrice

I woke to the sound of someone moaning at the top of their lungs and frowned. That darn Kerri was doing her thing again. No, it couldn't be Kerri. It sounded like her, but her bedroom was right above mine and this sounded like it was coming from Paul's apartment. I smiled when the person moaned again. It was Kerri, all right. She was just in Paul's apartment. I knew she was gonna fuck him when she found out about him winning the lottery.

I got out of bed and saw that Jordan had already gone to work. He'd said something about doing overtime to try and bring in some extra money. Fine time for him to try to help, now that he had gambled away all the rents.

I had plans of my own this morning. I was gonna go down to the bank and see if I could work something out, like maybe a payment plan. It wasn't like we didn't have any money. We had a grand, and I figured a little was better than none. I quickly showered and put on one of my business suits. I grabbed all of my paperwork and made sure I had the look of a professional black woman who had it all together, rather than the broke, desperate woman that I was.

"Good morning, I'd like to speak to Mr. Hawkins, if at all possible." I smiled at the young clerk.

"I'll see if he's available. And you are?" she asked.

"Katrice Taylor," I answered, and she walked to one of the back offices. She was gone a few moments. Then she returned with a short, balding man with a gray moustache.

"Mrs. Taylor, how are you this morning? Come on back to my office."

I followed him to a small office and had a seat. I looked around nervously and watched as he clicked his computer.

"Well, let's see. I am quite sure you know the status of your account at this point. Are you here to make a payment?"

"Yes, I am. But, Mr. Taylor, I don't have the full amount," I said slowly.

"Well, how much of the payment do you have? Maybe we can work something out." He smiled nicely. I was glad to hear him say that. I had already calculated that the money for Paul's and our rent totaled two grand. Plus Jordan had deposited four hundred and my own paycheck was eleven hundred.

"I have thirty-three hundred right now."

"Three thousand is a far cry from ten, Mrs. Taylor. Have you spoken with your brother about this?" He frowned at me.

"My brother is out of town on business, Mr. Hawkins," I lied. "I am trying to contact him, but he's a very busy man."

"That's understandable. I'll tell you what. You make the payment of three thousand three hundred today, and I will give you a sixty-day extension on the balance. How's that?"

"That would be great! Thank you so much." I stood and shook his hand.

"You're very welcome. Your father was a good friend of mine." He nodded.

I walked back into the lobby of the bank and advised the teller I needed to make a payment out of my checking account to the mortgage.

"Yes, ma'am, just fill out this transfer slip and I'll be happy to do it," she said. I filled out the small white paper and signed it, passing it back to her. Her fingers flew across the keyboard and she frowned at the screen. "Mrs. Taylor, I can't make this transfer."

"What do you mean? Why?"

"There aren't enough funds available." My heart began to race as she slid the form back to me.

"There's over three thousand dollars in that account. My direct deposit just went in two days ago and I haven't written any checks," I told her.

She pointed at the paper. "The balance on this account is only two hundred forty-seven dollars, ma'am. There have been several ATM withdrawals on this account in the past few days."

"How? I have both ATM cards right here." I was fuming by now.

She looked at her computer and pressed a few more buttons. "Last week we issued a third card on the account to your husband. I'm sorry." She truly looked sad.

"No, he's the one that should be sorry." I was livid. "Close the account. Transfer whatever funds are left to the mortgage and please add this." I handed her the rent money I'd collected. She handed me a receipt. "Tell Mr. Hawkins I will call him later."

I stormed out of the bank and fought back the urge to scream; I was too mad to cry. I headed right for Jordan's job. Only he wasn't there. He'd been fired over a week ago. So I knew where he'd be. He'd be at home.

I scared the shit out of Jordan as I burst through the apartment door.

"Shit! What the hell are you doing home?" He jumped off the couch.

"No! What the hell are you doing home?" I jumped in his face and pointed my finger with attitude. "And why are all these mother-fuckers in my house?" I looked in my living room and saw Rodney and about five or six other guys crowded around my living room floor. I couldn't believe Jordan.

"Aw, baby. They cancelled overtime today and I left." He sighed. "Me and the fellas was just having a little bit of fun. Right, guys?"

"Get the fuck out my house, all of you!" I told them.

"Aw, Trice, why you gonna do that? I was on a roll. Just chill and let us finish up, yo." Rodney gave me this pleading, almost desperate look.

"No!" I yelled, pointing to the door. "Now I'm about to call the police. Anyone here when I hang up the phone will be considered breaking and entering. Not to mention gambling." Everybody in the room scrambled to get out, including Rodney.

I went into the room and looked over at the chair where Jordan usually threw his uniform. It was empty. I looked on the back of the closet door and there it was, hanging where I put it after I cleaned up the day before. For some reason I hadn't noticed it earlier. I snatched it down, took it into the living room, and threw it at him.

"What the fuck is your problem?" he asked, clearly embarrassed.

I didn't answer him. I walked into the kitchen and reached under the sink, grabbing a trash bag. I rolled my eyes at him as I passed him and remained silent. I opened the dresser drawers and began to fill the bag with his clothes. He had to go. I heard him come into the room and felt his hand on my arm, trying to stop me.

"Trice! Trice! What the hell are you doing? Put my shit back!"

"Don't touch me, you lying, no-good bastard. What the fuck did you do with my motherfuckin' money?" I remained focused on what I was doing. I had worked so hard and given so much. For what? So this nigga could throw it all away. I was better than that.

"Trice, wait, baby. I was tryin' to win it back. I was tryin' to get the money for the building. I ain't steal it. I was borrowing it."

"You stupid-ass boy! If you took it from my ass without permission, that's stealing! And why the fuck was I gonna loan your ass money to gamble? You lost all our other money. I want your ass outta my building and outta my life! How the fuck you gon' gamble in our house, Jordan? You've gone too far now. I am sick and tired of this shit."

"Trice, baby, please! Don't do this. I love you, Katrice. Don't do this!"

"Get out, Jordan! Get out, now!" I was screaming at the top of my lungs and I no longer tried to hold back the tears. I picked up the full bag and rushed to the front door. I opened it and threw it out. The bag burst before it hit the ground and all of his clothes spilled on the sidewalk.

"What the hell are you doing, Katrice? That's my shit!" He ran out to pick his stuff up. I went back inside and slammed the door, locking it behind me. I fell on the sofa and cried until my eyes were swollen shut. I heard someone knocking on the door.

"Go away, Jordan!"

"It's not Jordan. It's me, Paul. I heard the commotion. You a'ight?" Paul asked as I cracked the door.

"Yeah." I sniffled.

"Mind if I come in?"

"No, but I'm not gonna be much company."

"You never are anyway." He smiled and I shook my head, opening the door. He followed me into the living room and we sat on the sofa.

"I look crazy, huh?"

"Nah, you looked crazy a few minutes ago when you damn near hit me with that big-ass bag of clothes, though."

"You saw that?"

"I was standing right in front of you." He smirked.

"I'm sorry, Paul. I didn't see you." I couldn't help but smile. Paul was a good guy and my best tenant.

"Anything I can do to help?"

"Can you pay your rent for the next year in advance now that you won the lottery?"

"What's really going on with the building, Katrice?"

I sat and told him the entire story from the reading of the will to what I had just found out in the bank. "And to think I wanted to have a baby by that gambling, bad-luck nigga. I guess my baby would've had to survive off forties and whatever he won at the craps table."

"That wouldn't be much."

"Seriously, do you think you can float me a loan to save the place?"

"Look, Katrice, there's something I have to tell you," he said. He sounded like he might be getting ready to say no, and I panicked. I just started talking, hoping I could say whatever he needed to hear to agree to the loan.

"Paul," I interrupted, "if it's a matter of paying you back, don't worry. Once I get back on my feet, I'll make weekly payments to you until we're straight."

"No, it's not that."

"Well, what is it, then?" I was so desperate.

"How much do you owe, Katrice?"

"Ten thousand."

"Oh, okay." All of a sudden his mood seemed to brighten. "I can definitely do that for you. And don't worry about paying it back."

"No, I can't do that. I want to pay you back, Paul."

"Look, Katrice, you just give me a few months free rent and we'll call it even, okay?"

"Thank you so much!" I jumped up and hugged him. "You have no idea how much this means to me."

"You deserve it, Katrice. You're a good woman," he told me. "I gotta go take care of some business right now, but when I get back we can sit down and talk about the details, okay?"

"Thanks, Paul." I smiled as I walked him to the door.

"I'll be back in a couple of hours. Get all the paperwork on the building together so I can go over it with you."

"Okay," I said, and closed the door. *Funny*, I thought, *Jordan's been out of my life for five minutes and my luck has already changed for the better.*

12

Paul

I walked out of Katrice's place, ready to head downtown to handle my business, when Rodney stepped out of his apartment.

"Yo, Paul. Let me talk to you for a minute."

I walked over and stood about four feet away from him. "Whatcha want, Rodney?"

"Look, now that you rich and shit, I was wondering if you could hit me off with a loan. You know, to cover some shit."

I looked at him and I had to laugh. The nerve of this guy. Here he was, this supposed baller that I didn't even get along with and he was coming to me looking for a loan. What'd he think I was, stupid? He wasn't buying no drugs with my money.

"What the fuck's so funny?" he snapped.

"You are, Rodney. Do you really think I'm gonna loan you money so you can buy drugs and kill our people? You must be out of your fucking mind." I turned to walk away.

"Who said it was for drugs?"

"Then what's it for?" I folded my arms and waited for a response.

He hesitated, then told me this cockamamie story about some guy named Big Red who was gonna kill him if he didn't give him fifteen grand by tomorrow. The damn story was so stupid, it made me wanna give him the money even less than before.

"So if this story is true, why don't you just go to the police?"

This time he laughed. "You don't go to the police on a guy like Big Red Logan. "

"Why not?"

" 'Cause then he'll kill your entire family." Rodney looked like he was actually starting to get upset. Either he was for real or he was a great actor. "Look, man, you gonna loan me some money or what?"

"Let me ask you a question, Rodney. Why do you owe this Big Red guy so much money? Is it drug related?"

He didn't answer my question. "Look man, you gonna loan me the money or what?"

I shook my head. "Nah, sorry, man. I can't do it."

"You can't do it? You got fifty million and you can't loan me fifteen thousand?"

"Nope. I can't do it. It goes against everything I believe in."

Rodney started to breathe heavy and his features got tight with anger. I figured I was about to be in a fight, but that wasn't a problem because I was sure I could kick his little ass.

"Everything you believe in? Everything you believe in? Motherfucker, do you believe in living?" he shouted as he reached in his coat and pulled out a nine-millimeter handgun. He pointed it right at my chest. "If you don't wanna loan me the fifteen thousand, then I'll take the whole fifty million. Where's the motherfucking ticket? And get them fucking hands up!"

I put my hands up like he asked.

"I asked you nicely because I didn't want any trouble. But you don't seem to understand." His voice was actually trembling as he waved the gun at me and spoke through clenched teeth. "Now I'm desperate and I'm sick of being nice. This ain't no game, Paul. These motherfuckers ain't playing. They mean to kill me."

"Put the gun down before you hurt someone, Rodney." I tried to keep my voice calm. I didn't believe he really wanted to shoot me. Like he said, he was just desperate, and desperate people do whatever it takes to obtain the objective.

"I'm gonna hurt *you* if you don't give me that motherfucking ticket." He was starting to sweat and his hands were shaking. That wasn't a good sign. He might pull the trigger by accident.

I tried to buy some time. "Look, Rodney, I don't got the ticket on me. It's upstairs. I'll give you my keys. Why don't you go up there and get it?"

"What do you think, I'm stupid? You expect me to believe you'd just leave a fifty-million-dollar lottery ticket upstairs where someone could steal it?"

"It's the truth."

"You fucking liar!" He hit me with the gun and I stumbled backwards a few steps. "Now stop playing games and tell me where the ticket is."

I touched my head and I was bleeding. I suddenly became very afraid.

"Oh shit! What the fuck you doing, Rodney? Robbing 'im?" We both glanced at the front door and Jordan was standing there with a big-ass smile on his face.

"Jordan! Quick! Go get the cops!" I yelled.

"Man, fuck you. I'm not going nowhere. This is an opportunity of a lifetime. Yo, Rodney, you want me to search him?"

Both Rodney and I looked at Jordan like he'd lost his mind, but Rodney still held the gun on me.

"Search him for what?"

"For the ticket."

"Huh?"

"Hey, man, you can't get away with this without some help. I can help you. Fucking Paul is big and it's gonna be hard hiding his body without making people suspicious. Now, I got a car and I know this place upstate where we can bury him and nobody will find the body. What do you say, partner? We gonna get paid?" Jordan gave Rodney a devious smile. I couldn't believe this shit. I knew Jordan was an asshole, but I never would have guessed he was capable of something like this. This whole thing was getting more serious by the second.

"Partner? What, you want half?" Rodney frowned.

"Nah, man, that wouldn't be fair. You the one with the gun. I just want ten million. That leaves you with forty mil. What do you say to that?"

"Jordan, you motherfucker!" I cursed. "I'm gonna whip your ass when this is over."

"Shut the fuck up, Paul. Don't nobody talk to my partner like that." Rodney sneered. "Search his pockets, Jordan."

"So we got a deal?" Jordan grinned.

"Yeah, we got a deal." Jordan started going through my pockets, but a female voice stopped him cold.

"Hold up! If you gonna give him ten million, I know you gonna give me ten million." We all turned to the stairs where the voice was coming from.

"Kerri? Not you, too!" I shouted. "You're not gonna sell me out, too?"

"You damn right, I'm selling you out. You may have some good dick, Paul. But I told you, you was gonna regret that shit this morning." She turned to Rodney. "I want ten million just like Jordan. You cut me in, and the only other person who even knows Paul had the ticket is Katrice."

"Man, don't worry about Katrice. Once I show her that check for ten million dollars she's gonna say, 'Paul who?' " Jordan assured everyone. It wasn't very reassuring to me, though.

They all laughed, but I didn't see a damn thing funny. These people were really gonna kill me over a lottery ticket!

"A'ight, Kerri, you in for ten mil," Rodney decided. "Go check the front door. Make sure nobody comes in." She ran to the front door while Jordan finished going through my pockets.

"It ain't here," Jordan told Rodney.

"Whatcha mean it's not there?"

"It's not in his pockets," Jordan replied.

"Where the fuck is the ticket, Paul? I'm running out of patience with you."

"I told you. It's upstairs in my apartment." I prayed he would believe me this time.

"Where in your apartment?"

I hesitated in answering and he lifted the gun to my head. "It's on my dresser," I stammered. "You can't miss it."

"You got his keys?" Rodney asked Jordan without taking his eyes off me.

"Yeah," Jordan answered.

"Then go get that ticket. And Jordan, if you ain't back in five minutes, I'm gonna shoot Katrice."

"Man, I'll be back."

Jordan took off up the stairs, and in a flash it seemed like he was back.

"You find it?"

Jordan smiled. "Yep. Right where he said it would be."

"You know, Paul, you a fuckin' fool to leave that shit sitting all unprotected in your apartment. Someone could try to rob you or something." Rodney laughed at me.

"A'ight, let's go," he announced to his partners in crime. The next thing I knew everything went black.

13

Katrice

"Thank God" was all that I could say after Paul left the apartment. I knew he was a good guy, which was why I'd tried to hook him up with Kerri. I just had no idea how good.

I went into the bedroom and got my lockbox out of the top of the closet. It held all the paperwork from the bank and receipts from when I had gotten various repair work done. I kept all the legal paperwork in a safe deposit box across town. I didn't know if Paul needed to see it, but I decided to go and get it anyway. When I walked out of the building he was talking to Rodney. I was going to tell him I'd catch up with him when I got back, but he seemed pretty preoccupied.

I was on cloud nine the entire ride to the bank and back, thinking of how God always shows up right on time. He even kept Jordan out of my way. Which was a surprise because I expected him to be waiting for me when I got home. I climbed the steps and knocked on Paul's door, but there was no answer. I looked at my watch and made sure two hours had passed.

"His business with the lottery office must've taken him longer than he thought," I said to no one. I went back downstairs and tried to think of some way to kill time while I waited. I looked around my cluttered bedroom. With Jordan gone it was gonna be a lot easier to keep this place clean.

I pulled the sheets and comforter off and threw them in the laundry basket. *I may as well wash these.* I grabbed a handful of quarters and tossed the detergent on top of the linens, pulling the rickety basket down the basement steps. I opened the washing machine top and put the quarters in the dispenser. I heard something moving in the storage closet at the back of the room and jumped.

"Who's there?" I called out and waited for an answer. My heart was pounding and I could feel beads of perspiration forming on my temples. I looked around for something to use as a weapon, but there wasn't even a stick to be found.

"Is someone in there? 'Cause I've got a gun and I ain't afraid to use it!" I yelled and took a step toward the stairs.

"Mmmmmm! Mmmmm!" someone moaned.

"If this is a joke, it ain't funny! Now get out of there before I call the fucking police!" I said as I got closer. I figured it was probably Freddie sleeping off his high.

"Freddie? Is that you?" I kicked the door with my foot and heard something scraping against the floor. I didn't know what the hell to think then.

"Ahhhhhhh!" I screamed and pulled the door open.

I meant my scream to scare whoever was in the closet, but I was the one who got spooked. When the door swung open fully, there was Paul, gagged with some tape and tied to a chair. Sweat was dripping down his face and he had a knot on his head the size of a grape. His shirt was wringing wet and his eyes looked crazy.

"What the hell happened to you?" I asked. He tried to talk but it came out like a muffled moan. I carefully tried to pry the tape off, but he still wound up screaming like a girl when I yanked on it.

"Owwwww. Come on, Katrice, we gotta get out of here before they get back! They're crazy! And they're gonna come back to kill me!" He panted and struggled to get untied.

"Who's crazy? What are you talking about?" I attempted to help him get free, but he was tied too tight.

"Your husband Jordan—"

I cut him off. "Jordan? What's he got to do with this?"

"Him, Rodney, and Kerri! They're trying to kill me. You gotta help me, Katrice. They knocked me out and robbed me!"

"You lying!" I fumbled with the rope.

"Do I look like I'm fuckin' lyin'? Rodney pulled a gun on me and they jacked me for the ticket! They gone down to cash it in right now and then they gonna come back and kill me. Trust me." He scooted the chair in frustration. "We gotta go call the cops and get out of here before they get back. Come on!"

"Jordan?" I asked. "Are you sure?"

"Yes, I'm sure! He's in cahoots with Rodney and Kerri. They're all in it together. Come on. We gotta hurry before they get back!"

I finally got the knot loose enough so Paul could get free. He jumped out of the chair and grabbed my arm as we ran out of the building.

"I can't believe they took the ticket."

"Believe it. But boy, are they in for a surprise." He shook his head.

14

Kerri

"Yo, we're almost at the lottery office, y'all," Jordan announced with excitement.

I can't begin to tell you how anxious I was to get that money. I was gonna take me a long vacation, then buy a penthouse apartment right here in the city. No more relying on men to pay my bills for me. I was gonna live footloose and fancy-free and do *me* for once.

"Hey, Jordan, what you gonna do with your money?" I asked.

"I'm gonna buy this racehorse I've been looking at. I'm gonna get him the best trainers money can buy so I can win the Belmont and sit in the winners' circle." He smiled.

"Don't racehorses cost a lot of money?" Rodney asked.

"This one only cost three million."

"Man, once you pay for the horse, the trainers, and stables, you ain't gonna have shit left."

"The purse for winning the Belmont is a lot of money. I'll be okay."

"What if you don't win?"

"Just the thought of having my own horse in the Belmont and being able to bet on him will be worth every dime. Besides, who said I wasn't gonna win?"

"With your bad luck, you couldn't win if he was the only horse." Rodney laughed. Jordan looked hurt, so I changed the subject. No need for any problems before we got our money.

"Well, what about Katrice? Aren't you gonna buy her anything?"

"I'm gonna pay off the building for her. That's the only thing she seems to care about."

"Man, you crazy. Katrice is a good woman. What you need to do is give her half of what you get," I advised.

"She's right, Jordan. The way you gamble, you just gonna fuck that money up."

"Yeah, well, we'll see," Jordan replied. Which meant, "Not a chance."

"What about you, Rodney? What you gonna do?" I leaned over the front seat.

"First I'm gonna go pay Big Red back. Then I'm gonna buy my mom a brand-new house. Nothing used in it. She never had any new shit 'cause she was always buying for us."

"Ah, that's sweet," I told him, "but what about you? Are you gonna buy anything for yourself?"

"I'm thinking about going down to the Bahamas or Jamaica and shit. Buy me a fat crib on the water and open up an import-export business."

"Damn, that sounds dope. Maybe I'll invest." I asked, "What you gonna export?"

"What else? Weed." We all laughed with Rodney, but it wasn't really funny.

"Damn, Rodney," I asked, "have you ever thought about going legit?"

"No," he told me flatly, and I sat back in my seat.

"We're here," Jordan announced, pulling into an open parking space. We all piled out of the car and tried to stay calm as we walked into the building, following the sign to the lottery office.

"How you doing? We'd like to turn in the winning ticket to Thursday's lottery." Rodney smiled nervously at the woman at the counter.

"This past Thursday?" she asked.

"Yeah, the fifty-million-dollar jackpot." I could barely stand still, I was so excited. I shuffled back and forth, wishing I could dance, I was so happy about this money. I was about to become rich.

"Wait here one minute. Let me get my supervisor." She walked away, then returned with a well-dressed brother in his early forties.

"You said you have the winning ticket for last Thursday's lottery?" he asked in an official tone.

"Yeah," Rodney replied, shoving the ticket across the counter at the man.

The man looked at the ticket strangely, then put it into a machine before calling over another man. I looked up at the ceiling. I guess I expected balloons and confetti to drop out of it.

The brother whispered in the white man's ear, then the white guy inspected the ticket and did all the talking from there. "Sir, this isn't the winning ticket." His voice was a mixture of formality and pity. Like he thought we were a bunch of fools or something.

"Man, that's bull!" Jordan yelled. "It's got the right numbers, don't it?"

"Yes, sir. It does, but—"

"Then I'm not leaving here without my money," Rodney snapped, cutting him off before he could finish. He was patting his jacket like he was about to pull out his gun or something. I grabbed his arm like I was his girl.

"Calm down, Rodney. You, too, Jordan. Let's hear the man out." I was afraid that Paul had escaped and called the cops or something. Maybe this was some kind of setup before they locked us all up. But if it wasn't, it was best if we didn't cause a scene up in here. I asked in my most polite voice, "Now why are you saying this isn't the winning ticket if our numbers are correct?"

"Like I was about to tell your friend, miss, your numbers were right for Thursday's lottery, but your ticket was purchased on the Friday after the numbers had already been announced."

"What?" Now I was losing my cool, too. "That can't be right," I snarled.

"Here. Look for yourself. The date is for Friday the seventeenth. Obviously whichever one of you purchased this ticket was playing some kind of game. Perhaps you all want to discuss this amongst yourselves, away from the window?" He crossed his arms over his chest and let us know we were dismissed.

I took the ticket from him and literally screamed. "Oh my God, Rodney, he's right!"

Rodney snatched the ticket out of my trembling hand. He took one look at it and started to walk out of the lottery office. "I'm gonna kill that motherfucker."

Jordan and I were right behind him. I don't know what Jordan was thinking, but I was about ready to offer to help Rodney pull the trigger when we saw Paul again. That motherfucker had planned this whole thing. He bought that ticket *after* the winner was announced, for one reason only. And me? I'd stupidly played right into it. Gave up the ass without even thinking twice. Now Paul was gonna have to pay, 'cause no matter how good his shit was in bed, no one makes a fool out of me.

15

Paul

"Let me ask you something, Paul," Katrice said to me as we sat in her apartment, peeking through the blinds. We were waiting for Rodney, Jordan, and Kerri to return. I'd told her everything about the ticket being a fake, so we both knew they'd probably come back here looking for me, upset. But we were prepared for them.

"What is it?"

"If you never had the winning lottery ticket, why'd you tell me you could help me save the building?" she asked.

"Don't worry about that. It's not fifty million, but I did recently come into some money."

She smiled at me and turned back to the window just as Jordan's car pulled up in front of the building. All three of them jumped out of the car, and I can tell you there was no doubt they had blood in their eyes.

"Dear God, Paul, you were right! Rodney's got a gun." Katrice's hand flew to her mouth.

"I told you."

I moved from the front window to the front door peephole when they walked up the steps, so I could watch as they walked right into our trap. The cops had shown up after we called them, and were waiting in the entryway, guns drawn. Rodney was the first one to come through the door, and his eyes got huge when he saw the cops. It didn't take long before his gun was on the floor and his hands were behind his back. Kerri broke out into tears. Jordan just raised his hands.

Once all three of them were handcuffed, the police knocked on Katrice's door and we stepped out.

"You ain't never had the winning ticket, did you?" Rodney growled at me as I stepped into the hallway.

"Nope. Can't say that I did." I was smirking as I answered him.

"You did all this just to get some ass?" Kerri sniffled.

"Actually, Kerri, I did this all because I hoped that if you got to know me, you'd forget about the money and see what kind of a person I am. Money's not a big deal to me. I found fifteen thousand dollars in the laundry room last week."

"Fifteen thousand dollars? That's my money!" Rodney snapped. He looked like he was struggling to get loose from the cop, who was still gripping his arm.

"I kinda figured that out after you had Freddie in the garbage looking for a brown envelope." As soon as I'd found the money, I knew it was his. And I also knew where it had come from, so there was no way I was returning it to Rodney. Since I volunteered at a rehab clinic, I knew firsthand what drug dealers like Rodney were doing to damage our community. I'd planned on turning the envelope over to the police, but then Katrice came to me that day and told me she might lose the building. So I kept it just in case. Katrice was a good black woman. If I could use Rodney's drug money to do something good for a strong member of our community, then that's what I was gonna do.

"You motherfucker!" Rodney screamed.

The cops led Rodney, Jordan, and Kerri out of the building, and Katrice and I followed. She didn't even seem too upset when they put her husband in the back of the police car. I know I was happy to see them drive away.

As the police car disappeared around the corner, a long, black limousine pulled up in front of the building. The driver stepped out and ran to the back to open it. A well-dressed man, who appeared to be in his early fifties, stepped out.

"Paul! Paul!" the man shouted as he approached.

"You know him?" Katrice asked. Her eyes lit up a little. Poor Katrice. She knew I was gonna help her out with her debt, but she still had to worry about getting new tenants in a hurry. So I guess any connection to money was looking good to her right then. I felt bad I couldn't say I knew the guy in the limo.

"I never seen that man in my life," I told her. But the man's voice *did* sound familiar.

"Paul! Paul! It's me, Freddie!"

"Freddie?" I stared at him. "Oh my God, Katrice. It's Freddie!" I laughed.

"Freddie, what you doing all dressed up and clean-shaven?"

"We hit, Paul!" he yelled with a hearty laugh. "We hit the fifty-million-dollar lottery. I told you I had the numbers."

"Damn! Congratulations, Freddie," was all I could manage to say. After the day I'd had, I was pretty much speechless.

"No, congratulations to you." He handed me an envelope and I opened it.

"Freddie," I said slowly, "this is a check for twenty-five million dollars." I heard Katrice gasp next to me. Maybe I could help her after all.

"I told you if you loaned me that two dollars and I hit, I was gonna split it with you."

Ghetto Fabulous

Angel Hunter

Acknowledgments

I would like to acknowledge GOD, my strength and my provider in all that I do.

"Ghetto Fabulous" is dedicated to the single moms doing their thing and holding down, sacrificing, advising, crying, denying, loving, wondering, questioning and doubting. You make me proud to be a woman and a mother and I applaud you.

The unconditional love and support of my son, Anthony, and the father of my son, Tony Irby, gives me the strength and courage to continue following my dreams and I thank you.

Thanks again to my good friend and mentor, Carl Weber. You go, boy!

Angel Hunter
Selfofessence@aol.com

1

The Present

My eyes were closed and I had a big-ass smile on my face. I'd just had the orgasm of my life.

"Do you know how much I love you?" my husband asked after we finished making love. Even though the act was complete, I could still smell him on my body and feel him inside me. No, not because his dick was just that big, but because of how intense the lovemaking was.

I didn't want this morning to end, but I knew it was just getting started, and would get better. Today was the beginning of a new lifestyle, a lifestyle of the rich and famous, ghetto style.

"Yes, I do, and I love you, as well." It felt so good to say those words freely, without fear or doubt behind them. It had taken me a while to get to this point and now that I had, I felt complete.

"I'm the luckiest man on earth."

"That you are," I joked.

"You've got a big day ahead, are you excited?"

"You know I am," I told him. Actually, "excited" was an understatement.

I was dropping my children off at private school, going to the spa for a day of beauty with my sister, and having the grand opening for my hair salon, Champagne and Shampoo. Not bad for a girl from the 'hood, an ex–welfare recipient.

Champagne and Shampoo was my dream come true, a hair salon that served cocktails in the back. You may be wondering where I came up with this idea. Well, ladies, we know how long you can be in the hairdresser's, waiting impatiently to get your hair done. We all hate it, admit it.

The hair salon that I used to go to, allowed the clients to bring in bottles of liquor, as long as you kept it in your purse, to sip on and pass the time.

So instead of sneaking, I figured why not have a place where you can do both out in the open. The salon in the front and the bar in the back. Of course, I went through hell to get a license, but with the help of my hairstylist turned partner, Aisha, whose uncle was the mayor of the town, I got it.

Climbing out of bed, I kissed my man on the lips and said, "I'm going to jump in the shower."

"Want me to join you?"

I wanted to say yes but knew it would delay me getting my day started, so I turned the offer down.

I arrived at the spa an hour and a half later; my sister was waiting in the lobby. We greeted one another with a hug. It felt so good seeing her look healthy.

"You look good," I told her.

"Thanks to you."

"Thank yourself, you did the work."

Our names were called out, interrupting our sister moment. We went to the front desk and were given towels, slippers, and keys for the lockers. We were told to follow the young lady waiting in the hall to the back, to change clothes, and our treatments would begin.

Ten minutes later, I lay on a table, relaxed, waiting on my massage. I closed my eyes and thought back to less than six months ago, when my life was a mess. When I thought that I would just continue struggling with my relationships, my friendships, and my finances.

Little did I know a dream about numbers and a little bit of luck would change my life. What happened? I hit the lottery. Can you believe that shit? Me, a young black girl from the 'hood, who one day decided, what the hell, and bought a ticket, was now a multimillionaire. Life doesn't get any better than this.

2

Six Months Ago

"Please just get out my face, go outside and play, do something, damn." These kids were getting on my nerves. I wish Tyrone would come and get their asses so I can get a break. I'm tired of his ass coming and going when he feels like it. Next time he steps through this door, I'm going to let him have it. At least I think I am. I can't get on his case too much, because he does take care of all three of my kids, and only one is his.

"Girl, when we gonna go out? We haven't done our thing in a long time," Shantay asked while puffing on a cigarette.

"You need to put that cigarette out; you know I don't allow that shit in my house," I told her sorry ass while rolling my eyes. All she wanted to do was go out and party, like she had nothing better to do. I don't get it. This bitch has three kids and every single one of them has been taken away by Social Services because of her drug habit. You would think that alone would make her get her life together and try to get her kids back, but hell no, she feels "freer to do her thing." I don't know why I put up with her ass. I'm lying, I do know. She's my sister, and if I don't love her, no one else will, including herself. I feel like I have to look out for her.

"Shantay, instead of worrying about going out, what you need to be doing is going to a NA meeting and looking for a job, so you can get your kids back."

"You and those meetings, you think that ever since you started going there, you're better than me. Well, let me tell you something, you're not. We come from the same womb, missy." While telling me a thing or two, she smashed the cigarette out on my plate.

"You know what, you're trifling. Do you hear me, straight up. I'm just trying to help you out."

"I didn't come over here to be helped out or to get a lecture; I just came by to see my niece and nephews. I'm out of here," she told me and jumped up, ready to walk out the door. I just looked at her, not about to stop her. I already had a headache and her leaving would relieve it just a little. She's lying anyway; the real reason she came over is to borrow some money. I knew it and so did she, so the second she walked through the door, I went into my "I'm broke as hell" routine.

"All right then, 'bye."

She walked out of the house, slamming the door behind her. I lay across the couch, said a quick prayer, and hoped the kids wouldn't come back in the house for another hour or so. I needed time to think and evaluate my life. Where it is now and how I got here. Isis Bray is my name, I'm a mother of three at the ripe young age of twenty-seven, no husband, unemployed, on welfare, and disgusted.

That's right, disgusted, with me because I allowed myself to be put in this situation, because I allowed myself to get caught up out there, because I allowed my life to go down the drain, and I'm tired of getting sucked in. I'm tired of living below my means. I didn't have anyone to blame other than myself.

And yes, you heard me right, I did say three kids. One girl, she's ten, I had her when I was seventeen, and two boys, six and four. Ain't that some shit. I still can't believe it. I've got my hands full. I have to be honest and tell you that yes, they all have different daddies. Don't go thinking I'm a whore or anything, because I'm not; I was in love, or what I thought was love, with the first two fathers, and the last one was a mistake, a welcome one.

I'll tell you a little bit about the first two no-good daddies. Queen, that's my daughter's name, her father's name is Understanding. You heard me right, Understanding; he's a five-percenter, a God (at least that's what he thinks) in the Nation of Islam. I met him when I was fourteen and in the ninth grade. I'd just entered high school, he was eighteen, a senior and fine as hell. I had the biggest crush on him. When I think back on it now, I have to laugh at myself about how I use to follow him around and leave love notes in his locker. He knew I had a crush on him, too, because he would tease me by saying, "Just wait until you turn sixteen." I thought he was playing, so I never asked him what would happen when I did. I just continued to lap after him, meaning you could see my tongue hanging on the floor when he walked in a room.

3

My Babies' Daddies

Understanding lived around the corner from me and drove a motorcycle. Now you know that made him the man even more. I had built him up to movie-star status. His partner in crime, Dwayne, lived right next door to me, so my head was always out the window. Whenever I heard a motorcycle, I would run to the window and look out, hoping to catch a glimpse of him. This went on for two years.

Eventually I turned sixteen and he was twenty. That night my mother was letting me have a party at my house, and it was going to be off the hook. My sister's boyfriend was a deejay and she talked him into making some tapes for me. Since I was considered one of the popular girls in school, it was a sure bet that everybody who was anybody would come.

Prior to that day, I dressed like a tomboy, always in jeans and T-shirts. I would refuse to wear skirts and dresses, but since it was my birthday my sister convinced me to wear a skirt. When I looked in the mirror, even I had to admit that I looked rather good.

The party was packed. I was dancing with one of the guys on the football team when a slow song came on and I felt a tap on my shoulder. Turning around, I was surprised to see Understanding with flowers and a gift in his hand.

"Happy birthday, beautiful," he said while handing me my gift.

I was flustered and surprised.

"I know I wasn't invited but didn't think you'd mind."

"Of course I don't mind, I didn't invite you because I didn't think you would come."

"Well, I'm here and you're sixteen."

"Yep, sure am."

"You know what that means, right?"

"No, what?"

"That I can take you out now."

The smile I gave him must have spread across my whole face. Finally, I was going to go out with him. It would have to be on the sneak tip, though, because my mom would surely freak once she found out. Especially with him being twenty, a grown-ass man. I was ready to leave my party that second if it meant I could be alone with him.

"So when do you want to take me out?" I asked him, trying to sound like an adult, and sexy. I think I even batted my eyes.

"Whenever you're ready."

"I'm ready when you're ready."

"How about I pick you up from school Monday and we'll hang out afterwards."

"I have to do something after school. How about we hang out during the day."

"What about school?"

"What about it?" I was being bold as hell. I knew I would have to cut school. Shantay would look out for me; I'd looked out for her plenty of times.

"Girl, are you out of your mind?" Shantay asked me Sunday night, when I told her my plans about not going to school.

"No. I like him, that's all, I want to chill with him."

"He's too old for you."

"Why you gonna be like that? I thought you was my friend."

"I *am* your friend. I'm just saying, he's too old and too experienced for you to be playing with. You're sixteen and still a virgin."

"So what's that got to do with anything?"

Rolling her eyes, Shantay said, "You cannot be that naïve. Understanding would like to get in them panties, it's as plain as day. Why else would a twenty-year-old be interested in a sixteen-year-old?"

"How about because I'm cute, because I'm nice, because he knows how long I've liked him. If all he really wanted to do is have sex with me, he would have tried to get it a long time ago, but he didn't. So now, talk what you know and not what you think."

"You're stupid. I can't believe you honestly think what you say is true. I know that no matter what I say, you're going to do what you want to do. I won't rat you out to Ma, but remember he's a man and you're not yet a woman, so instead of trying to be grown, you need to be careful."

It was too late for that. I already knew that he would be the one I gave my virginity up to. All my friends were doing it and it was time for me to do it, as well. I was ready and willing and I wanted Understanding to be the one.

Monday finally rolled around and I had him meet me on the side of the school. He was driving a Jeep Wrangler.

"Ohhh. Whose Jeep?" I asked while climbing in.

"Mine. I picked it up this weekend. You like it?"

"Of course."

He eyed me up and down, then placed his hand on my thigh. "You look nice."

Blushing, I told him, "Thanks." I had on my sister's black miniskirt, no stockings, some pumps and a white T-shirt with my name across the front. I'd shaved my legs for the first time that morning.

He started rubbing my thigh. "So how does it feel to be almost grown?"

I laughed and said, "It feels nice."

"Where do you want to go?"

"I don't know. Wherever you want to go."

"You want to go to my house?"

I knew he lived with his father. The rumor was that his mother left them for another man. "Where's your father?"

He looked at me with a smirk and said, "He's away, not that it matters. We don't get in each other's way."

"Well, let's go," I said in a bolder tone than what I felt.

When we reached his house, I followed him inside and we went into the kitchen.

"Are you hungry? Want me to make you something to eat?"

I was too nervous to eat so I told him no.

He sat across from me at the table and smiled. "You're pretty, why don't you have a boyfriend?"

"How do you know I don't?"

"Are you saying you do?"

"No."

"Have you ever had one?"

"No." I looked down at my hands.

"Have you ever had sex?"

"No."

He didn't say anything after that. Not wanting to turn him away, I looked up and told him that I wanted him to be my first. Just like that, put it on the table, no beating around the bush or anything.

"Are you sure?"

"Yes."

Standing up, he told me to go sit in the living room, turn on the television, and that he'd be right back. I did as he instructed, and after about ten minutes he reappeared and said to follow him.

We ended up in his bedroom, where he'd lit candles and had some Bobby Brown playing in the background. I was scared out of my mind, ready to run out of the house. My mind was telling me no, to leave, but my body was telling me yes, to stay.

Understanding took my hand and led me to the bed. We sat down. "Don't be scared. I'll be gentle," he told me, and leaned over and started kissing me. I'd kissed three boys prior to him but those kisses were nothing like his. He did things with his tongue I didn't know could be done. I found myself moaning and reaching over to touch his penis through his pants. It felt big. I also could feel myself getting moist.

Standing up, Understanding told me to lay back. I did, and he proceeded to undress me. He started licking and sucking on my nipples, then he headed toward my stomach and I felt his tongue between my thighs. I jumped up and tried to push him away.

"Wait, wait."

Looking up at me, he laughed and said, "Relax, baby, you're going to like what I'm about to do. I told you I'd be gentle and I meant it. I'm going to make your first time like the movies."

I believed every word he said. I allowed my body to relax. I told myself to not be so uptight. When he put his tongue inside me, I swear I thought I was about to cry. I felt this wave come over me; it felt like I was in the ocean and being carried out to sea. The next thing you know, I was screaming out loud and he was taking his clothes off and climbing on top of me.

"It's going to hurt at first, but you'll get use to it."

I looked down at his penis and panicked. There was no way that was going inside me. I immediately tightened up.

"Don't tighten up, relax, kiss me."

As he pushed inside me, tears fell down my cheeks; I fell in love, and he knew he had me from that moment on.

For the next year I was a woman possessed. I couldn't get enough of him. I wanted to be with him every day, every second. I lived and breathed that man. He dogged me out, too. I would get into arguments and fights over him with older women and girls my age. I was out of control.

Finally I devised a plan to keep his ass, and that was to get pregnant. I thought if I had his baby, then surely he would treat me right. For a while, he did just that. I don't know what it was. Maybe it made him feel more like a man that he was going to become a daddy. Whatever it was, all he talked about was the fact that I was carrying his seed and he was going to teach his son this and teach his son that. I was in my glory; he got us a little apartment with the money he was making from dealing drugs, and convinced me to get Section 8 and welfare.

"I'll take care of you. You don't have to work, but you can still get paid by the system and have a little extra spending money," he told me.

He was my master and I was willing to do everything he told me to do. It was as if I was a puppet and he was pulling all the strings. The day finally came when I went into labor and he was nowhere to be found. My mother, who was dying from cancer, and my sister, who by now was getting high occasionally, were like, "I told you so." The thing is, they did; they kept saying that Understanding wasn't any good, they kept questioning what kind of man would make his woman get on welfare, and finally when he didn't show up for Queen's birth, they just straight out told me I was stuck on stupid. He showed up three days later, all apologetic and shit. I was too tired to argue. I went through hell with that man.

For two years, I put up with his bull, and my only escape was when he got busted and thrown in jail, where he remains for ten years on charges of possession of drugs with the intent to distribute.

My second child's name is Trey Jordan (TJ for short) and his daddy Trey Senior was a piece of work. When Understanding got locked up, I swore off relationships. I didn't want to be bothered with another man. I was going to school trying to get my GED, because I'd dropped out following behind Understanding's ass and just taking care of Queen.

I met Trey at my daughter's ghetto-ass day care. I hated leaving her there, but it's what Social Services paid for. Trey would be there picking up his son. I have to admit, I'd noticed him before and never spoke because his son's mother was always with him, and she would give me the evil eye. I was about tired of that. I had made up my mind that the next time she looked at me wrong, I would say something.

Well, the day finally arrived when I'd had enough; my sister was getting on my last nerve. The night before, she came over and asked me to baby-sit her daughter for a couple of hours. I said yes and her ass never came back. It's a good thing her daughter, Kenta and Queen went to the same day care or I would have missed class. I'd got into an argument at school with Understanding's sister, YoYo, who wanted to know how come I never took Queen to see her father in jail. I told her it wasn't any of her fucking business. I wasn't and didn't plan on taking Queen to see him in that place. It wasn't because I was being a bitch, it was because the one time I did take her, there were two other girls there to see him and one of them had a kid with her around the same age as Queen whom she claimed was Understanding's. I didn't have time for the nonsense.

Anyway, by the time I got to the day care I was fed up and ready to bust someone upside the head. I went to sign Queen and Kenta out and bumped right into Trey.

"Excuse me," I told him.

"That's okay," he replied.

I went to walk around him, but he wouldn't move.

"Um, can you move out of my way?" I asked with irritation in my tone.

"As soon as you tell me your name."

I looked over his shoulder and asked, "Where's your girlfriend, I'm sure she'd want to know my name, too."

"We broke up."

"You were just here together yesterday."

"And?"

"And you expect me to believe that you broke up?"

"Damn, girl, all I asked you for was your name. If I thought it was going to be all this, I wouldn't have." He turned to walk away but I stopped him.

"It's Isis."

"I'm Trey."

After that day we would talk for a few minutes each time we saw one another. He would ask me out and I'd say no. I was trying not to get involved with anyone. Eventually loneliness got the best of me and I accepted his invite. That invite turned into another, and the next thing you know he'd moved in with me and I was pregnant once again, this time with TJ. Why didn't I have an abortion, you may wonder. I don't know, only thing I can say is the thought never crossed my mind.

Trey was the total opposite of Understanding; he didn't cheat on me, he doted on me with affection and attention, never material things. As a matter of fact, I started noticing that he never had any money. I didn't understand it, he worked as a manager in a tele-marketing firm and there was no reason for him to be broke all the time. He didn't have to pay any rent, I was still on Section 8 and collecting welfare, so we should have been living large. Well, I got my answer one day when I was doing laundry and felt something in his pockets.

What I pulled out shocked me: cocaine, wrapped up in aluminum foil. I started to flush it down the toilet but decided to try it instead. That was the worst thing I could have done, but I didn't know it at the time.

I had two girlfriends, Lisa, a newly acquired friend, and Dana, a childhood friend, whom I chilled with occasionally and they both did cocaine. They were always talking about how good it made them feel, how they would have all this energy and be amped up. They claimed the sex was better when they were high and they would clean the house from top to bottom. They offered it to me a couple of times but I'd always said no. By now Shantay was doing drugs heavily and had given birth to a little boy that was born addicted. He was taken away along with my niece.

I know that sounds fucked up, the fact that I let my niece and nephew get taken away, but I felt like they weren't my responsibility and that maybe this would make Shantay get her act together.

Well, the day I found the cocaine I was tired, had been cleaning and taking care of my son and daughter, I had to cook something to eat, and just wanted to lay my ass down. I thought about what Dana and Lisa said about cocaine making them feel like Superwoman, and decided to try it. I wanted to find out what it was about this drug that turned people out. I figured I was mentally strong, I knew better, it wouldn't have the same effect on me.

I went into the kitchen and poured some of it on the table, making lines like I'd seen them do with a matchbox, cut up a straw, and sniffed some up each nostril.

"Oh shit!" I said out loud. It burned the hell out of my nose and went straight to my head. After rubbing my nose a few times, I took a couple more hits and waited to feel a surge of energy. After a while my heart started racing and I started sweating. I was paranoid. I stood up and started pacing the floor, threw some water on my face, and sat back down. My daughter and son were in the living room watching a movie while I went through the motions of the first high.

That day I cleaned the house from top to bottom and cooked the best meal of my life. By the time Trey arrived home, I had finished what was in the aluminum foil and wanted more. The question was how to get him to get some for me. After all, I wasn't even supposed to know that he was doing it.

"So, Trey, how was your day?" I asked him as he sat down to eat.

"Fine." He looked around the house and said, "The house looks nice."

"Thanks, sweetie."

After a moment of silence, I asked, "Trey, what do you do with the money you make?"

Looking up, he said, "Huh?"

"I didn't stutter. I asked you what you do with the money you make."

"What do you mean, what do I do with the money. I buy things for you and the kids. I pay child support to Kim and don't get to see the child that I'm supporting."

Kim, the other baby's mama, hated the fact that we were living together, and would play games with Trey's other son and Trey visiting him. I told him to take her ass to court, but no, he didn't want to listen to me. He kept saying he had it under control.

"So you're sitting there telling me that you spend it on me and the kids?"

"That's what I said."

"Well, tell me this, when is the last time we went shopping? When is the last time we went out to dinner? When is the last time you bought me something just because?" I was getting worked up.

"Where is all this coming from?"

Not able to hold it in any longer, I reached into my pocket and threw the aluminum foil on the table. "I found this in your pocket when I was doing the laundry."

He didn't say a word. He just looked at it.

"I think this is where your money has been going."

Trey looked at me with the saddest eyes. "Baby, I'm sorry. I don't know what to say."

Pissed and high, I said, "You don't know what to say, you don't know what to say. Here you are getting high with money that could be used to better us and you don't know what to say."

I almost felt bad for him because of the look of regret. "I tried it," I blurted out.

This caught him off guard. "You what? You did what?"

"I said, I tried it."

Suddenly he was up on me. "Give it to me now."

I backed up and told him no.

"What the hell is the matter with you? Why would you do something like that."

"Why would I do something like that? Why the hell would you?"

This conversation was not going the way I wanted it to. My goal was to get him to go and purchase more, but instead we were arguing. I needed to change the way this conversation was going. "Listen, I don't want to argue about it. I don't have a problem with you getting high every now and then, I just wish I didn't have to find out this way."

He was looking at me, stunned.

"As a matter of fact, if you're going to get high, we might as well do it together."

I put the package on the table and paused for a second or two. I was waiting to see if he was going to stop me. A part of me was hoping he would, but that didn't happen.

"Well, let's do this," he shocked me by saying instead.

"You ain't said nothing but a word?"

He stood up, reached into his pocket, and pulled out another package.

That was the first time we got high together, and afterwards the sex we had was mind-blowing. All inhibitions were down, but afterwards I have to admit I regretted it. Regretted the whole thing. Regret didn't stop us from doing it again.

Now we all know this situation wasn't going to work for long; it could, would, and did only go from bad to worse.

It seems like the second it was out in the open, Trey went crazy with it. Every day he would come home wanting to get high, even when I didn't want to. It was getting—no, it had gotten out of control.

What was the breaking point, you may be wondering. Well, there were several. We tried to keep what we were doing from the kids, either making sure they were asleep or not in the room with us when we were getting high. What we didn't count on was the fact that the kids didn't need to see us getting high when they could imitate us instead. They started walking around sniffing and rubbing their noses. One day, Queen was cutting up straws.

"What are you doing?" I asked her, startled, hoping she wasn't doing what I thought.

"Cutting up straws. I see you and Daddy doing this all the time."

I almost started crying. Only reason I didn't was because I was high at the time.

Another time we stayed up all night getting high, didn't even take the kids to day care, Trey called out of work, and we got nothing accomplished. My sister came over that day, took one look at us, and had the nerves to call us trifling, skank-ass negroes.

"I can't believe this shit. I can't believe that you're getting high."

Of course I denied it. "Ain't nobody getting high. I don't know what you're talking about."

"Yeah, okay. I'm not stupid, I know when a person is high as hell, and you are, you and that man of yours. I thought you were smarter than me."

I was so glad Trey was in the bedroom and couldn't hear us.

"Look at me, look at me, do you want to be like me? My kids were taken away, I'm pregnant again, and this one will probably be taken away, too. Do you want to end up like me?"

Shantay went on and on, ranting and raving. Sooner than later what she was saying started to sink in. I could lose my kids, I was turning into someone I never thought I'd be. I'd allowed cocaine to get the best of me.

The next day, tired and hungover, I told Trey we needed to talk.

Well, I talked and he listened. I told him we needed to stop getting high, that not only was it destroying us as individuals but that it was destroying our family, as well. He agreed. Long story short, agreeing to make a change and actually making a change are two very different things.

I called the 1-800-Cocaine number and they told me about NA meetings, which I started to attend. Not only was it hard but it was embarrassing, as well. My pride didn't get the best of me, though. I stuck it out.

As I attended these meetings, I started to change for the better, but Trey was getting worse in his addiction. He'd even lost his job. I kicked him out, had no choice. I have to admit that sometimes I think about him; I can't help it, he was good to me. I use to wish things had turned out differently until I'd see him hanging on the Avenue, the spot where all the drug dealers and drug addicts hang, and I knew I did the right thing.

After Trey, I really swore off men. Then how did I end up with child number three, you ask. It's called horniness and a failure of birth control. By now I'd smartened up and got on the Pill. I'd been without sex for months when I finally accepted an invitation from Tyrone for dinner.

Tyrone and I met at the grocery store. I had the kids with me and was struggling with the bags when he came over to the car and asked if I needed any help.

"I'd like that," I said, not even trying to play the strong woman role.

As he started to place the bags in the car, he turned to me and said, "Haven't I seen you at the meetings?"

I didn't have to ask what meetings he was talking about. "Probably."

"Well, I'm Tyrone."

We talked a little, and the next thing you know he invited me to dinner. We had sex that first night, and two months later I found out I was pregnant. The damn Pill failed me. It's rare when it happens, but it did. By the time I figured out I was pregnant, I was eleven weeks and there was no way I was heading to the clinic. I can remember being scared to tell Tyrone. I didn't want him to think I tried to trap him. When I did tell him, he took it in stride; he even went so far as to take some of the blame by saying maybe he should have worn a condom.

Tyrone and I still see each other occasionally; he takes care of his son, my baby Malik, and what I like most about him is he doesn't forget my other kids. He sometimes takes them places and buys them things. He doesn't have to do this but he does. He often talks about us being together, but I'm afraid to enter into another relationship; the first two went down the drain, plus right now I think I just need to concentrate on me and trying to get my life together. I just finished beauty school and registered for the LPN class, and well, I need to give love a break.

So now, here I am with three kids, still on welfare, working under the table at a salon, and trying to do my thing.

4

It's Party Time

"Girl, come on and go out with us tonight. We're hitting Club Onyx."

I was on the phone with Dana. I wanted to say okay because I hadn't been out in so long, but when you've got three kids it's hard to just up and be like, all right. Dana only had one child, a daughter, so it was easy for her to get a baby-sitter.

"I don't know. I have to try and get a baby-sitter and you know that's easier than it sounds."

"Don't worry about it, bring the kids over here; my niece is staying the night, pay her a few dollars, and she'll baby-sit."

"Are you sure?"

"Yeah."

"Ask her while I'm on the phone." I had to have Dana do that, because she'd tell me it was okay and I'd get there and her niece Tina wouldn't know a thing about it. Believe me, it's happened before.

"I said it was okay."

"Let me speak to your niece. Put her on the phone."

"Damn, girl, you don't trust my word?"

Laughing, I said, "No, as a matter of fact I don't."

She put her niece on the phone and I asked her if she wouldn't mind watching the kids if I'd pay her.

"Oh, so you're asking this time," Tina said and I could just imagine her hands on her hips.

"Now you know the last time wasn't my fault, that was your aunt."

"Mmm-hmm."

Getting frustrated and feeling like I was begging her ass, I said, "You know what, forget it."

Popping her teeth, she said, "I'll watch them. I don't mind. Shit, your three kids act better than Dana's one."

"I heard that," Dana said in the background.

"I wasn't exactly whispering," Tina told her.

Interrupting their little tit for tat, I thanked her and asked her to put Dana back on the phone.

"See, I told you she'd say yes."

"Yeah, okay."

We talked some more about what we were going to wear and hung up. I was excited as hell. Like I said earlier, I hadn't been out in a long time and was ready to get my groove on. This was going to be my celebration of finishing beauty school and starting nursing school.

I fed the kids and told them I was going out.

"Well, where are we going?" Queen asked, always the outspoken one.

"Tina's going to watch you."

"Oh, I like her."

Whew, I was glad to hear that, because if tonight went well, I planned on taking my ass out a little more. Sometimes I get so lost in this motherhood thing that I forget I'm young and should be enjoying myself.

I let the television baby-sit the kids while I showered and got dressed. I decided to wear a basic black strapless dress that fit my hips and behind just right, and stopped just above the knees. I put on some black heels that tied up the leg and pulled my hair back into a ponytail. Glancing in the mirror, I smiled, liking what I saw. Shit, having three kids didn't do too much damage.

Grabbing my purse, I gathered the kids and drove over to Dana's. It was time to party and a sister like me was ready.

"Oh, girl you look nice," Dana said when I walked in.

I wish I could say the same about my girl. She could not dress. There was a time when I would have said something, but it always fell on deaf ears. One time she even told me I was just jealous. I let it drop after that. I decided to let her dress how she wanted to. Tonight, for example, she wore this tight white unitard. Now you know white don't look right on everybody, especially a thick sister, and Dana was most definitely that. You could see every bump, hump, and lump.

"Thanks," I told her, as I got my kids settled and gave them each a hug and kiss.

"Let's take my car," Dana said, when we stepped outside.

"Fine with me," I told her, thinking we were hopping in her Jeep Cherokee, but when we stepped outside and she started walking over to a Lincoln Navigator, I had to stop in my tracks.

"What the hell, or should I say who the hell's Navigator is this?"

"Girl, Ricky bought this for me."

"Ricky? The drug dealer Ricky? Please tell me you are not messing with that knucklehead."

"That and then some," she said, laughing and climbing into the car.

I started to give her a lecture on dealing with thugs and how it won't get you anywhere, when she threw up her hands and said, "Please, Miss Holier Than Thou, no lectures. I'm grown and having the time of my life, he treats me and mine good, I don't want, ask, or need for anything, and I'm going to take advantage of it while it lasts."

Well, at least she knew that it wouldn't. So I just said, "Be careful."

"Words from the wise," she replied while putting the key in the ignition.

When we pulled up to the club, the haters were definitely out. We stepped out of the Navigator and immediately the women in line starting cutting their eyes at us. I didn't want to wait, either, because I felt something would go down if we did and I was too old for the nonsense.

"Dana, let's go somewhere else, I don't feel like waiting in line."

"Girl, please, ain't nobody got to wait. The bouncer at the door is Ricky's friend." She grabbed my arm. "Come on."

I let her lead me to the front of the line, ignoring all the heckling that was coming from the other women.

"How are they just going to walk up in the front?"

"I know he's not going to let their asses in."

"Oh, hell no."

The women were pissed. I have to admit, I would be, too, if I was waiting in line, but you know what, I wasn't.

When we got inside, Dana turned toward me and asked, "You want a soda or juice?"

She knew that I didn't drink anymore; that came with not doing drugs. The first time we went out and I ordered a soda, I thought Dana was going to lose her mind.

"What the hell are you ordering a soda for, you can't get a drink like everyone else?" she asked.

"You know I'm going to those meetings now." I didn't try to hide it from my crew; if we were going to continue being friends, they had to respect my choice.

"Yeah, but I thought that was for cocaine not for liquor. You didn't have a problem with drinking."

"It goes hand in hand," I told her.

All night she bothered me about it, trying to force my hand until finally I left the bar without even telling her. When she arrived home that night, she called and asked me, "What's your problem?"

"Listen, you know I'm trying to get my act together. If I make a decision and you can't respect it, I don't need to hang out with you anymore."

"Oh, so it's like that?"

"It's exactly like that."

She hung up on me. We didn't speak for at least two weeks, and one day I came home from picking the kids up and there was this card taped to my door. It was from Dana, saying how sorry she was, that she loved me, respected my decision, supported my choices, and that she had my back.

Now when we go out, she respects my wishes.

Lisa, on the other hand, I had to cut off. She didn't give a freak about anyone other than herself. Now, she knew where I stood as far as drugs and shit go, and that wench had the audacity to bring the shit up in my house.

I had a birthday party for Malik and invited Dana, her daughter Danielle, Lisa and her kids, along with a few kids from day care. I noticed that Lisa had slipped off somewhere and had been gone for a while. Her children were acting out, and not one to discipline someone else's kids, I went to look for her.

Lo and behold, she was in my bedroom with the door locked. I'm not stupid; there weren't any men at the party, so I knew she wasn't in there getting her freak on.

"Open the door," I told her.

It took her a good minute or two to open the door. When she did, I glanced around the room and didn't see any evidence of what I suspected, but when I looked at her face, it was all on her nose. I almost went upside her head. I didn't need to see that shit, it was already bad enough I was taking this sobriety thing one day at a time, and this day was one in which I was struggling through.

"I know you're not disrespecting my house like this."

Of course she tried to play it off. "What are you talking about?"

"Go look in the mirror and you'll see what I'm talking about."

She did and just smirked, wiped her nose, and said, "Oops, my bad."

"I think you need to leave."

She started laughing.

"I'm not laughing, Lisa, I think you need to leave. I'm not having this up in here. Get your kids and get out."

"Oh, so it's like that."

"It's exactly like that."

Well, she got her kids and left.

You might think I was a little harsh with her but a sister has to do what she has to do. I was trying to change my life and I couldn't have people in it that didn't respect what I hoped to accomplish. After Lisa left the party, Dana asked me what happened and I told her, so she knew I wasn't playing. She never got high or talked about getting high in front of me or with me again, although she did get her drink on. That didn't bother me.

We were sitting at a table in the back of the club, me drinking a ginger ale and Dana, a Cosmopolitan. The music was banging, so I found myself dancing in my seat.

"Ohhh, look, girl. That fine brother over there is checking you out."

I looked in the direction she'd nodded her head, and fine he was. Tall, over six feet, chocolate complexion, wide shoulders, hair cut close, and dimples. I noticed those because he smiled at me. Of course I smiled back.

"He's coming this way, girl. He's coming this way," Dana teased.

I just started laughing because she is so silly sometimes.

"Get him, girl," she said and stood up.

"Where are you going?" I asked.

"I'm going to let you and Mr. Man get to know one another."

Before she could walk away, he was upon us.

"Hello, ladies, can I get you a drink?"

Dana sat down real quick and said, "I'll have a Cosmopolitan."

"I'll have a ginger ale," I told him.

He looked at me with surprise.

"I don't drink."

"I don't, either, so I'll have a ginger ale with you."

He waved one of the waiters over, ordered our drinks, and sat down.

Looking at me, he asked me my name.

"Isis, and this is Dana."

"I'm Lavert."

"Is that your first name?"

"Yes, people always ask me that."

"I've never seen you here before," Dana told him.

"This is my first time, I'm here for a game."

"A game?" Dana asked.

"Yes, I play for the Nets."

Dana started kicking me under the table. I know that was her way of saying, *Snatch him up with the quickness.*

"Oh," I said, unimpressed because I don't watch sports and it wasn't a big deal.

"You like basketball?" he asked, all his attention on me.

"No, not really, I'm too busy working and taking care of my kids."

Dana kicked me again. She hated when I did that, mention my kids so soon. She said it scared men off. I didn't care because I felt a person needed to know from the door what was up. I don't want to waste anybody's time or have mine wasted, either.

"How many kids do you have?"

Before I could answer him, I heard Dana say, "Oh shit." She wasn't paying us any attention; her eyes were glued to the door. I looked to see what made her say that, and to my surprise, or should I say to my horror, Understanding was walking in the door with Ricky.

My heart started racing. I was scared, nervous, and ready to get up out of there before they spotted us.

"Excuse me, I have to go to the ladies' room." I stood up.

"I'm coming with you," Dana said.

We scurried away. We couldn't leave the table fast enough.

* * *

Inside the ladies' room, I kept repeating over and over, "Oh my God, oh my God."

"When did he get out?" Dana asked.

"I don't know. I want to leave, I'm not ready to see him yet."

"And what is he doing here with Ricky?"

"Come on, we have to leave." I don't know why, but I was panicking. Understanding had been calling me collect for the last two months, and I hadn't accepted any of his calls. This must have been why, to let me know he was coming home. I hadn't taken Queen to see him in three years. I just gave up on the whole thing. It was tiring, and I kept getting into confrontations with his other child's mother. I knew he was scheduled to be released soon but I had no idea it would be this soon.

Sensing my stress, Dana took my hands and said, "Listen, Isis, there is no way we're going to get out of here without his seeing us, and I'm sure Ricky saw the Navigator in the parking lot. So you have to get it together and handle this. Plus, you've got that fine-ass basketball player waiting for you at the table; the least you can do is go tell him 'bye and give him your number."

I knew she was right; I couldn't hide from Understanding. Now that he was home, we were bound to run into one another. Taking a deep breath, I said, "Okay. Let's go."

We walked out of the bathroom and headed toward the table where Lavert was waiting. I sat down and Dana didn't. "I'll be right back," she said.

I knew she was going to try and distract Ricky and Understanding while I handled my business.

"Lavert, I have to leave. Thanks for the drink."

"You have to leave so soon? You just got here."

"I know, but I called home and the baby-sitter had an emergency."

"Well, can I see you again?"

"Ummm . . ."

Reaching inside his pocket, he pulled out a card. "Call me."

Before I could respond, I heard the voice from hell. "Isis baby, how you doing?"

I looked up to find Understanding. Dana was behind him mouthing, *I'm sorry.*

Lavert stood up and said once again, "Call me."

I didn't say a word. I was scared to because Understanding was looking at Lavert like he wanted to kick his ass.

"Excuse me," I said, standing up, trying to brush past him. "Dana, are you ready to leave?"

Dana looked at Ricky, who had an amused look on his face. "Yeah."

Understanding still didn't move. "How's my daughter?"

"She's fine."

"How's my pussy?"

Ugh, I hated him. "I wouldn't know; ask one of those ho's that were visiting you in jail."

He laughed and said, "Still feisty, I see."

I tried to move past him again. "I have to get home."

"To call the basketball player?"

"It's none of your business."

"I can make it my business."

Dana, tired of the nonsense, said, "Damn, Understanding, let the girl go."

He looked at her and told her to mind her business.

Dana looked at Ricky and said, "You're going to let him talk to me like that."

Ricky told her she did need to mind her business, that this was between Understanding and me.

"I'll be by tomorrow to pick up my daughter," Understanding informed me.

"No, you won't."

"You can't stop me."

I wanted to smack him so bad my hand itched, but I knew that this was not the place to cause a scene. It was already bad enough people were looking our way.

"Understanding, please don't do this. You haven't seen her or talked to her in over three years, and you expect to come home and act like nothing's changed, like it's all good. It's not that easy."

He didn't hear a word I said. "I'll see you and my daughter tomorrow." He bent over and kissed me on the cheek.

I wiped it off and he laughed.

"Come on, man," he said to Ricky.

"I'll be over after the club," Ricky told Dana, and we watched the two thugs walk away.

"Come on, let's go," Dana said.

I just followed her in silence.

Once we were in the car, I went off. "Can you believe him? I can't. He just thinks he's supposed to come home and see Queen, just like that. That it's supposed to be okay, and then he had the nerve to ask how's his pussy, like I belong to him. He dogged me out, Dana, does he think I forgot that? His daughter is ten freaking years old and she barely knows him. She's not some little girl who doesn't understand stuff, she's smart. I can't believe this shit."

Dana just listened. There really wasn't anything she could say, because this was my dilemna and we've both learned that when it comes to men, it's best to keep our thoughts and our advice to ourselves. In the end we end up doing what we want to do, and sometimes what we choose is the worst thing for us.

"You can't keep him from his daughter, Isis."

"I know. I know, but this is something that I have to get used to. His being home and all. Damn, I've got two other kids to think about, as well."

"What you need to think about is what Tyrone's going to say."

"Why?"

"That man is in love with you, girl."

She was right. He was in love with me. I just tried to ignore it. I knew he wanted more than I was giving him. Now, don't get me wrong, I care for him a lot, and like I said before, he's an excellent father. It's just that I've depended on men for so much for so long that it's time to depend on me.

"You can come get the kids when you wake up," Dana told me.

"Thanks."

When we pulled up to my house, my sister was sitting on my porch, or should I say nodding the drug on my porch.

"Damn, this night is just going from bad to worse."

"You want me to come in?" Dana asked.

"No, I got it." I climbed out the car and headed toward my high-ass sister.

"Hey, baby sis," she said when she saw me.

I ignored her and unlocked the door. She followed me in.

"I said, hey, baby sis."

"I don't have any money," I told her. I knew that's what she wanted.

"Did I ask you for any money? No, I don't think I did." Glancing around, she asked, "Where's my niece and nephew?"

"Over Dana's."

"Where you been?"

"Minding my business and leaving yours alone."

Shantay walked in the kitchen and opened the refrigerator. "What you got to eat?"

"Listen, I'm going to lie down, you need to take a shower because you stink, and then you need to take a nap. I'm sure you've been up for days."

"I don't have anything to sleep in."

"I'll put something on the couch," I told her and started to walk away.

"Isis."

Stopping, I faced her.

"Thanks for loving me."

"You're my sister, I'm supposed to love you." I hated when she pulled that sentimental shit on me. I went into my bedroom and closed the door behind me, threw myself over the bed, and cried myself to sleep.

The next morning, I woke up and peeked in the living room to see if Shantay was still there. Usually she'd sleep for a couple of hours and leave in the middle of the night. No such luck. She was sitting at the kitchen table, pen in hand, writing something. Curiousity got the best of me and I went over to her and asked her, "What are you writing"

"Girl, I dreamed some numbers last night and I wanted to write them down before I forgot them."

"Oh," I said.

"You should play them; I dreamed of three, you need to pick three more"

"Girl, please, I'm not playing no lottery, you and I both know that only old white people win. We don't stand a chance."

"Never say never, Isis."

"I think in this case it's safe to say it."

"Think about it, we might win."

I decided to play along. I asked Shantay, "If we did, what would you do with your part of the money?"

She got real quiet.

"What would you do?" I pressed.

"Get my kids back."

"Well, don't you think you need to get clean first?" That slipped out. I didn't mean to go there, it just sort of happened.

"Why you got to go and say some shit like that?"

"I'm sorry," I said, and in a way I was. Lately she's been talking about her kids more and more, so I knew it was a sore spot. "Okay, what else would you do?"

"I'd get the hell away from here, move someplace peaceful, go on a serious shopping spree. I'd buy up everything I've ever wanted and probably some things I don't need. I'd go to a spa once a week and just get pampered. I'd put myself in one of those real expensive rehabs, get clean, then I'd buy a car and go pick up my kids. What would you do?"

"First, I'd put some of the money away to invest, you know, do the responsible thing, because I have to think about the future. Money doesn't last, I don't care how much it is, after they take away taxes and stuff."

"Get to the good stuff, what would you spend the money on?"

"The first thing I would purchase is some red leather pants—I've always wanted a pair. Then I'd shop for my kids, take them to the toy store and let them rack up, get them computers and games, whatever they want, then we'd all go clothes shopping. I'd buy boots galore and get them a couple of pair of expensive-ass sneakers just because I can. Then we'd go to Disney World for, like, two weeks. I'd get a new car." I was just getting started and she cut me off.

"See, you have thought about it."

"I haven't thought about hitting the lottery, I've just thought about what I would do if I came into some money."

Shantay passed me the piece of paper with the numbers on it and said, "Come on, think of three more numbers and play them. Heck, it's only a dollar. If we win, I don't even want half, just a third."

I took the paper and put the children's ages down, just to appease her. Then again, you never know, they just might bring me luck.

"Now, was that so hard?"

I just rolled my eyes and started cooking some breakfast. "You want something to eat?"

"Yes."

I made us some bacon and eggs, called Dana and my kids, told them I'd be there within the hour.

Shantay borrowed something to put on and asked if I'd give her a lift to her room. I know you may be wondering why my sister isn't staying with me. Well, I can't have her in the condition that she's in around my kids. I told her if she gets clean, she can come live with me, so it's not like I didn't offer, but it's up to her to make the move, to initiate it. She hasn't yet, so there is really nothing I can or am willing to do other than love her from a distance.

5

The Past Will Catch
Up to You

I dropped my sister off at her room and went to get the kids. On the way there, my cell phone rang. I looked at the number and saw that it was unfamiliar.

"Hello?"

"What's up, it's Understanding."

I almost hung up the phone, but I knew that wouldn't do any good. I was going to have to face him sooner or later, and I figured why not now, over the phone, instead of face-to-face.

"How did you get my cell number?"

"I have my ways."

"Stop playing, how did you get the number?"

"Ricky got it from Dana."

I was going to curse her ass out. "What do you want?"

"I want to come and see my daughter today."

"I don't think that's a good idea."

"I don't give a fuck what you think. She's my seed just as much as she is yours, and you can't keep her away from me. It's bad enough you stopped bringing her to see me while I was on lock-down. I'm home now and I plan on seeing her when I feel like it."

This man knew how to get on my last nerve. Didn't he know you get more bees with honey?

"I have to prepare her first."

"Prepare her for what? I'm her father."

"You're not her father, a father does for his child."

"I couldn't do for her in jail."

"That's your fault."

"Listen, I know you've got a man."

"Who told you that?"

"His name is Tyrone. I know everything there is to know about you. Your second baby's daddy is a drug addict, you almost became one."

I hung up on his ass, didn't even let him finish. I also turned my ringer off in case he called back.

When I pulled up to Dana's house, I was going to let her have it. I walked in the house and looked around. "Where are the kids?"

"Tina took them to the store. They'll be right back."

I must have had a frown on my face because she asked, "What's wrong with you?"

"Why did you give Ricky my number to give to Understanding?"

Placing her hands on her hips, she asked me, "What the hell are you talking about? First of all, I wouldn't give Ricky your number, and I certainly wouldn't give it to him to give to Understanding. He must have gotten it off my Caller ID. So I think you owe me an apology."

"I'm sorry, I didn't mean to come out my face like that. It's just that he called me, demanding to see Queen. I hung up on his ass."

"You can't keep hanging up on him or walking away from him. You do know that, right?"

"I know."

"You're going to have to let him see his child sooner or later."

"I know. I know, but I want to be able to do it on my own time, when I'm ready, not when he's ready."

"If he knows your number, then he probably knows where you live."

Before I could respond, Tina and the kids walked into the house. "Did you kids have fun with Ms. Tina?"

"You mean Aunt Tina," Queen informed me.

I just laughed and said, "Yes, Aunt Tina."

"They always have fun with me," Tina said.

I paid her for watching them and told Dana that I'd call her later.

When I pulled up to my house, who was sitting on the porch? None other than Understanding. This was the last thing I expected.

"Stay in the car," I told the kids while climbing out. "What the hell are you doing here uninvited," I asked him with all the fury I could muster up.

"You hung up on me."

"So? I didn't appreciate you getting all in my business."

"I was just letting you know I know what you've been up to."

"And who told you my business, your nosy-ass sister?"

Understanding looked in the direction of the car. "Why did you leave the kids in the car?"

"Why do you think?"

Laughing, he said, "You really think you can keep Queen away from me?"

He started walking toward the car. Please God, I thought to myself, why is this man trying to cause a scene. I followed behind him, begging, "Please don't do this, not yet, give me a day or two to prepare her."

He paid me no mind. He had his hand on the door handle, the kids were all looking at him; even Queen had yet to recognize him.

"All right, I'll give you until tomorrow to talk to her. I'll be by around 8 P.M. and I'm telling you, you better be here."

"I will."

"I'm not playing, Isis."

"I said I'll be here. Now please, just leave."

He stood there looking at me for a second or two. Before walking away, he said, "You're still fine as hell, you know that, don't you."

I ignored this statement. I also didn't let the kids out of the car until he got into whomever's vehicle he was driving.

"Who was that, don't I know him?" Queen asked.

"Yeah, who was that?" the boys repeated.

I didn't answer them.

That night I lay in my bed trying to find a way to tell Queen about her father. Tyrone was in the room with the boys, reading them a bedtime story. Once again, he was staying the night. I found myself letting him do that a lot lately.

"So how was your day?" he asked when he came into the room and sat on the bed next to me.

"It was the day from hell."

"Why is that?"

Taking a deep breath, I told him, "Understanding came by here today."

Confused, he asked, "Queen's father? I thought he was in jail."

"Well, obviously he's out," I snapped, and felt bad immediately because there was no reason for me to be nasty to this man. All he did was ask me how my day went.

"You know what, I'm going to excuse the fact that you just snapped at me. You're upset."

"I'm sorry. You're right, I *am* upset. It was just a shock seeing him."

"What did he want?"

"To see Queen."

"Did you let him?"

"We'd just gotten home and he was on the porch. I made her stay in the car."

"What are you going to do about it?"

"What can I do? He's coming back tomorrow to see her. I can't keep him away from her. I begged him to give me a day to talk to her."

"Well, have you?"

"Not yet."

"Don't you think you need to?"

"Yeah." I stood up.

"You want me to come with you?"

"No, this is something I have to do on my own."

That was one of the things I loved but at the same time hated about Tyrone: he liked to talk about things, discuss and dissect. If left to me, I just keep it all in.

When I walked into Queen's room, I noticed immediately that she had my old photo album out and was staring at a picture of me, her, and Understanding when she was a baby.

"That was my daddy, wasn't it? The man that was on the porch this morning, the one you told to go away."

Damn, I thought I had put that photo album up.

"Why did you tell him to go away, Mommy? Was he here to see me?"

Sitting next to her on the bed, I was honest and told her, "Yes, he was."

"Then why didn't you let him?"

Wow, she wanted to know why I hadn't let her see him. How could I tell her that I didn't think I would be able to handle it? How could I tell her it was because I hated him and he broke my heart?

How could I tell her it was because of issues I had with him that had nothing to do with her? Kids are something else; they don't care about right or wrong, they just want to be loved.

It's obvious Understanding cared about her, because in reality, he didn't have to come over. He didn't even have to let me know he was home. When he saw me in the club, he didn't have to say a word to me.

"I don't know, baby, I didn't think you would want to."

"Why wouldn't I want to? Tyrone sees his daddy all the time, me and Trey never see ours."

What could I say other than, "He's coming back tomorrow."

She jumped up off the bed and went to her closet. "I have to pick out something to wear. I want to look pretty for him, maybe that way he won't disappear again."

It took everything in my power not to cry. I stood up and we picked out an outfit together—me praying that he would show up.

"So how did it go?" Tyrone asked when I climbed into bed next to him.

"She's excited," I told him, not really wanting to talk about it.

Opening his arms, he asked me for a kiss.

I gladly gave in. Maybe some passionate lovemaking was just what I needed to make me feel better. Tyrone is the best lover I've had. He is attentive, and eager to satisfy and please me. Even after four years, he made sure I was pleased and got mine before he got his. Who could ask for anything more? He would kiss and lick every part of my body. Why couldn't I love him back? Fear, plain and simple.

The following day, the kids and I went to the grocery store. While I was paying for my food, I pulled out the piece of paper with the lottery numbers on it. I started to ball it up when I thought, *What the heck, might as well play it.* What could it hurt? After all, the lottery was up to eleven million dollars. Like Shantay said, you never know.

I went into the pharmacy and played the numbers Shantay gave me along with the three I added. All the time thinking, *Who am I fooling? I'm not going to win.*

Walking toward my car, I was surprised to hear someone calling my name. I turned around and Lavert, the basketball player, was coming my way.

"Isis. How are you?" He looked even taller in the daytime.

"Wow, you're big," TJ said.

"So, these are your children?" He bent down to shake their hands.

"Yep."

Standing up, he asked, "So, how come you haven't called me?"

"I thought you were only in town for a couple of days."

"I was, but I'm back visiting. So, are you going to let me take you out to breakfast, lunch, or dinner?"

Thinking about Understanding's visit tonight, I told him it wouldn't be a good night.

"How about tomorrow?"

"I'd like that."

The kids were listening to every word.

"Do you still have my number?"

"Yes."

"Call me, okay?"

"Okay."

As I climbed in the car I felt all giddy inside. It must have shown on my face because Queen asked me, "Who was that?"

"Just someone I met."

"Do you like him?"

"I just met him, sweetie."

"Well, he likes you. I can tell."

"Okay, Ms. Observant."

"What about my daddy?" Malik asked.

I didn't answer him, I turned the radio on and up and drove home.

Queen was driving me crazy. Every five minutes she was asking me if her daddy would be here soon.

We waited and waited, eight came and went, then eight-thirty, then nine, and he still wasn't knocking on the door. Can you believe that? After all the mental anguish he put me through, he had the audacity not to show up.

I went from anger to heartache when Queen looked at me and asked, "Why doesn't my daddy love me, what did I do?"

I put my arms around her and told her, "You didn't do anything, sweetie. He does love you. That's why he insisted on seeing you today. Something must have happened."

I know I didn't make her feel any better because she moved away from me and ran into her room, slamming the door behind her.

I couldn't wait for Tyrone to get here because I was going to Understanding's sister's house to find out where the hell he was staying if not with her. You don't break my little girl's heart and expect everything to be okay.

I knocked on Queen's door. Not waiting for a response, I peeked inside and asked her if she was okay.

"My feelings are just hurt," she said.

"Can I come in?"

"I just want to be alone right now." She sounded just like a teenager, I thought to myself.

These kids today grow up so fast. When Shantay and I were growing up, half the stuff these kids said, knew, and did, we didn't know and weren't exposed to. Television is off the hook; with all the cursing and nudity that goes on, all you can do is tell your children that's not how you walk, talk, or behave, and hope they listen. All that bullshit about not letting your children watch television or listen to the radio is unrealistic. Motherhood is hard, especially when it's just one of you. Once I had children, it made me appreciate my mother even more.

Growing up, my sister and I didn't know our father, and I have to say that it had an effect on us. I know it did on me. I was always looking for love in all the wrong places. Trying to find that man that would give me what I thought was missing in my life. Understanding and Trey each had a part in them I thought my father might have. Understanding was strict, possessive, and always telling me what to do. That's what a father did, or so I thought. Trey was compassionate, loving, and thoughtful, he babied me—that is, until he got caught up out there. That's the type of father I wanted to have. Of course, at the time I didn't know that's what I was doing.

Whenever we asked about our father, my mother would just say, "He left us." As if that was all we needed to know. Well, he must have left and come back in time to get her pregnant again. I keep telling myself, I'm going to look for him, his name is on my birth certificate. I'm just afraid of what I might find. I sometimes wonder if I look like him at all, if he has other children, if I have any brothers and sisters walking around. How he would feel if he saw me. I know that I could relate to how my daughter was feeling—rejected and neglected.

When Tyrone arrived at my house that night, I told him about Understanding not showing up.

"So what are you going to do about it?"

"I'm going to run out and go over to his sister's to see if she knows where he's staying. Then I'm going to go confront his ignorant ass."

"Do you think that's wise?"

"Do I think it's wise? Hell, I'm not the one who started this shit. He's the one that came over here insisting on seeing her. I told him 'no' because I had a feeling something like this was going to happen. I'd rather not have him in her life at all than have him popping in and popping out."

"Are you sure about that? A child needs both parents."

"Yes, I agree with that, but a child can't be played with like a yo-yo either."

"How about I come with you?"

I touched his face. I knew he was trying to protect me, but I told him no, I wanted to handle this on my own.

When I pulled up to YoYo's house, the car Understanding had come over in was parked on the street. I hoped that meant he was here. I walked up to the house and banged on the door. There was music playing in the background. I knocked again; no one came to the door, so I peeked in the window and spotted Understanding on the couch with some skank-looking bitch sitting on his lap, giggling and shit. This pissed me off even more, so I banged on the window as hard as I could without breaking it.

This caught their attention. Understanding looked up at the window, and there I was, standing with my hands on my hips and a frown on my face.

Jumping up and snatching the door open, he said, "What the f—"

I didn't even let him finish, I just smacked him across the face. Once I realized what I'd done, I was ready to run, let me tell you. I didn't know what this man was or wasn't capable of anymore. But

I didn't run, I stood my ground. "Is this . . . this . . ."—I was pointing at the skank ho—"more important than your daughter? You come over begging me to let you see her and . . ."

The skank ho came and stood next to him, asking, "Who is this?" She had entirely too much attitude in her voice. I must have looked like I was about to smack her too, because Understanding told her, "Go sit your ass down."

She sat down and I continued on my rampage. "Like I was saying, you practically begged me to let you come see your daughter tonight and you don't even show up. She's home crying her little eyes out, talking about how come you don't love her, and what am I suppose to tell her?"

He opened his mouth to say something, but there was nothing he could say that I wanted to hear. I threw my hands up and said, "Nothing you can say will make this any better. You're here about to get your dick sucked and your little girl is home crying. That's the problem with you men, you say one thing and do the opposite."

Interrupting me, Understanding said, "Listen, let's just go now."

"Let's just go now? You think it's that simple?"

"I fucked up, Isis, what more do you want me to say? I'm sorry, damn. I do want to see my daughter. A brother just got his priorities a little mixed up, that's all. I've been on lockdown for almost seven years and got offered some pussy. What you think, that a brother was going to turn it down?"

When he said that foul shit, I was through. I looked at him with such disgust, I'm sure he felt it. "You know what? Forget you," I said and turned around to walk away.

He followed me. "Wait, Isis. Wait."

I ignored him.

"I'll meet you at your house. Okay, let me get rid of my company and I'll meet you at your house."

At this point I didn't believe a word he said. I just climbed in my car.

When I arrived home, Tyrone and Queen were sitting on the couch, the boys were gathered at his feet, and they were watching videos.

They all looked up when I entered. "How did it go?" Tyrone asked.

"It went," I said and kissed everyone on the cheek before going into my room to take a deep breath.

A short while later Tyrone came into the room and hugged me from behind.

I looked at him and felt something I didn't want to acknowledge—love. Damn, damn, damn. That's the last thing I wanted. Maybe I would go out with Lavert, to distract me from this emotion.

Looking at up him, I was about to say something when the doorbell rang. Together we walked into the living room to find Understanding standing with Queen.

"He came, Mommy, he came." Queen's voice was filled with such joy and excitement that I didn't have the nerve to tell him to leave.

Tyrone walked up to Understanding and told him, "Don't start anything you can't finish."

Understanding looked like he wanted to punch him in the face, so I stepped forward and told Tyrone, Trey, and Malik to go into the kitchen and leave Queen alone with her father.

"I thought maybe I could take her with me to my sister's," Understanding said.

"Oh, please, Mommy, can I go?"

Now that was one request I wasn't giving in to. "Not tonight, maybe another time."

"Why not, Ma?"

"Yeah, why not?" Understanding asked.

"Because I said so and that's reason enough. Now either it's in here, in my house, in my living room now, or it can just be another day in here, in my house, or not at all."

Tyrone grabbed hold of my hand and I realized my voice was getting louder.

"The choice is yours, Understanding," I said as I walked toward the kitchen with my crew behind me.

"When is my daddy going to come see me?" TJ asked.

This was the last thing I needed. "I don't know." I sat down at the table.

"Why don't the boys go to their room instead of sitting in here with us?" Tyrone asked.

While the kids were in their bedroom, I sat as close to the opening of the kitchen as I could to listen to what Understanding was saying to Queen.

"What are you doing?" Tyrone asked.

"What does it look like I'm doing? I'm listening to what he's saying."

"I can see that."

"Then why did you ask?"

"He's not going to hurt her, Isis. He just wants to talk to her."

I rolled my eyes at him and continued listening. From what I could make out, Understanding was telling her that he loved her but that where he was at, it wasn't a place for kids, that he was sorry, and that he would not be going back there, and he would make a better effort to be in her life. I couldn't hear her response because Tyrone was talking in my ear.

"Give the man a chance."

"I know you didn't just tell me to give him a chance, and you're the one who told him not to start something he can't finish."

I heard Understanding coming toward the kitchen and ran to the counter, trying to pretend like I wasn't listening.

Looking at Tyrone, he said, "Would you excuse us for a minute?"

Tyrone looked at me and I nodded.

When Tyrone was out of the kitchen, Understanding asked, "Did you hear enough?"

I was busted and unashamed so I said, "Yes, as a matter of fact I did."

"Listen, I apologize about tonight."

"Yeah, whatever."

"No, I'm serious. I want to do right by Queen. I'd like to come get her this weekend."

I looked at him like he'd lost his mind. "How about this, let's take it one step at a time. You can visit her, take her out, and we'll work up to the overnights."

To my surprise, he didn't argue.

6

The Winner

The next few days came and went. I decided to call Lavert to take him up on his offer of dinner, if he was still in town. Tyrone was getting next to my heart and I needed to distance myself.

Once again, I used Tina for a baby-sitter. Before going on my date, I went to my hairdresser, Aisha.

Now this girl could so some hair, let me tell you. She was the one who convinced me to go to beauty school, telling me it was easy, and plus, you could get paid under the table and still collect your checks. I wondered why she didn't have her own shop because she had most of the clientele at the salon.

When I pulled up, I saw Dana sitting in her Navigator taking a sip of tequila. It just so happens Aisha was standing outside smoking a cigarette and saw her. I was climbing out the car and Aisha tapped on Dana's window.

"Busted! You know you can bring that in here."

"Are you ready?" Aisha asked me as she went to her station.

When I made my appointment, I had stressed how important it was for me to get in and out, even told her I'd have a nice tip for her. So for the first time ever, I didn't have to wait.

"How she get to come in and get her hair done right away?" one of the other customers asked.

"Don't worry about it," Aisha told her.

While Aisha was doing my hair, she told me she was thinking about taking my advice and opening her own shop, that she was in the process of looking for backers.

"You go, girl. I told you, you should have done that a long time ago. If I had the funds, I'd back you."

We laughed and joked some, and when she was finished with my hair, I have to say, I looked finer than I already did.

"You look beautiful," Lavert said the second he saw me.

Instead of him picking me up, I decided to meet him at the restaurant. Okay, okay, I was scared that Tyrone would just happen to stop by at the same time. Not that we were officially a couple or anything, but I wanted to show the brother some kind of respect.

"Thanks, and you look handsome."

He did a GQ turn. "You think so."

Glancing around at all the other women staring our way, I told him, "I'm not the only one."

Acknowledging what I was talking about, he said, "I'm used to it."

He pulled my seat out for me and I sat down.

Dinner was nice. We talked a lot about his job and the traveling he did. How it affected his kids. He has two boys. We also talked about my kids. He didn't seemed turned off at all, at least not the way I expected him to be. As time went on, it seemed like he became more and arrogant; he kept talking about his money, his cars, and how women be sweating him. As quick as I found him attractive, with the same quickness I was turned off. It kind of made me appreciate Tyrone even more.

When it was time to leave, he said, "I'd love to see you again. I'm leaving tomorrow, but you have my numbers, use them."

"I will," I told him, lying.

Later that night I sat on my bed, smiling and feeling good about life. I would start nursing school soon. It's not what I really wanted to do, but with the new welfare reform, you have to take up some kind of schooling. I didn't know what I wanted to do, actually, other than raise my kids. I'd never really given having a career any thought. It was definitely time to start thinking about it. I enjoyed doing hair because I could do it on my time, but working every day in a salon, that wouldn't work with my patience.

The next day I dropped my kids off at camp and stopped by the grocery store on the way to the salon. I had an appointment but wanted to pick up something for lunch. While there, I heard some people talking excitedly. "Did you hear? Did you hear? Someone from this area won the lottery." I knew it wasn't me, so I didn't think about it.

At the grocery store, everyone was talking about the lottery winner, as well. "Whoever it was didn't come forward yet."

"Shit, if I won the lottery, I would have been at that store so quick collecting my damn money."

"I know, that's right. Me, too. I would have collected my money and disappeared."

Everyone had something they would have done, but ain't a damn thing any of them can do because none of them won the money. I didn't even put my two cents in. What was the use?

That night I was in my bedroom watching the news, something I rarely did, when they flashed the numbers on the bottom of the screen: 6, 30, 16, 10, 4, 42. I recalled adding my children's ages to the three numbers my sister gave me, and they were there. I couldn't recall the three she'd given me but I was curious. I never threw the ticket out, although I'd been meaning to.

I went into the living room and got my purse off the coffee table, and took out my wallet. I looked inside and pulled the lottery ticket out. I sat on the couch and turned the television on, waiting for the numbers to scroll across the screen again.

The numbers that flashed by were 6, 30, 16, 10, 4, 42. I looked at my ticket: 30, 16, 6, 4, 10, 42. I looked at the television. I looked at my ticket. I looked at the television. I must have done this for five minutes until it dawned on me that I had all the numbers.

Jumping up, I screamed and quickly covered my mouth, remembering the kids were asleep.

I couldn't believe this shit. This could not be happening to me. No, I was mistaken, there had to be some kind of mistake. I started pacing back and forth. Eleven million dollars, they said one winner. Could that be true, just one winner? Was I the winner of eleven million dollars?

Excitement, joy, and exhilaration were some of the emotions running through me.

I needed to tell someone, but who, who could I trust with this information? Dana? Tyrone? My sister? Oh shit, my sister. She picked out three of the numbers, was I obligated to give her some of the money? I paid for the ticket, sure, but I wouldn't have won without her numbers. Fuck, fuck, fuck, she was a drug addict. I couldn't give her the money. She'd go overboard with it.

I sat down, I stood up, I sat down. *God, somebody tell me what to do!*

The phone rang, startling me. "Hello?" I answered.

"Hello, is this Isis Bray?"

"Yes, it is, may I ask who's calling?"

"It's Jersey Medical. Do you know someone by the name of Shantay Bray?"

"Yes, that's my sister," I answered, my heart racing.

7

The Good and the Bad

I couldn't believe this, the best day of my life turned out to be the worst day of my life. I find out that I'm a freaking millionare and my sister almost overdoses. Maybe I was being tested or something, maybe this was a sign not to let anyone know just yet. Maybe . . . okay, okay, think—first I'd call Tyrone, have him come sit with the kids while I went to the hospital. I'd check on my sister and think about my next step, whatever that would be. Smiling, I thought, probably shopping.

Just as quick as that thought came, it went. I didn't have any right to be this happy, did I? Not when my sister, my flesh and blood was in the hospital. I didn't even know how serious it was. They told me I needed to get there as soon as possible.

Please, Lord, don't let her die. Please just let it be something minor. Now I would be able to send her to rehab, she'd get her kids back, life would be good. We'd move into a big-ass house together and live happily ever after.

When Tyrone arrived, I gave him a kiss on the cheek and thanked him.

"Call me and let me know what's wrong," he told me.

"I will." I opened the door and stopped. I wanted to tell him so bad about the ticket, but something stopped me. Right now just wasn't the time.

When I arrived at the hospital, I was shocked to find Trey Senior sitting in the waiting room. I almost didn't recognize him, he looked so worn. His clothes were tattered, he was unshaven and in need of a haircut. I thought about pretending I didn't see him but I couldn't do that; after all, he was my son's father. I hadn't seen him in over a year; I thought he'd disappeared off the face of the earth. I'm glad I was wrong, because although I was disgusted with the way he was looking, I was glad to see him living.

"Trey? Trey? What are you doing here?"

He looked up at me and smiled. "You look beautiful," he told me. "I still love you, you know, always will."

I didn't say anything. There wasn't anything to say because I use to lay up at night hoping and wishing he would come to his senses and realize that we were more important than drugs. It never happened. Even though I now knew he still cared, he was out of my system.

"I found Shantay passed out on Springwood Avenue and called the cops. I gave them your number to call you."

"How did you know my number?"

"Your sister gave it to me a long time ago, I was just afraid to call."

"Please don't leave, okay, stay here. I'm going to check on my sister, then I'll be back so we can talk."

Trey started shifting from side to side. "I have to be somewhere."

I knew he was lying, I knew he just wanted to leave the hospital to get a hit, so I promised him what I knew would keep him here: "Please, Trey, don't leave, I have money. I'll give you a couple of dollars to catch a cab to wherever you have to go."

That sat him down, like I knew it would.

I entered the room my sister was in, and there she lay, looking helpless.

"And you are?" the doctor asked

"I'm her sister. How is she?"

"She's a very lucky lady that the young man found her when he did."

I walked over to her and ran my hand down her face. Her eyes were closed.

"Shantay," I said, hoping she'd look up at me. "Shantay. It's Isis, sweetie, open your eyes."

She did.

"I'm going to leave you two alone. Just press the buzzer at the head of the bed if you need anything." He walked out.

Shantay looked at me and started crying. "I'm sorry, I'm sorry."

"Don't worry about it, it's okay. You're alive, that's all that matters." I climbed in the bed next to her and just held her.

"I can't do this anymore, Isis. I almost died out there. I just realized that I don't want to die, at least not by my own hands. I need help."

I was so glad to hear her say that, because as I lay there I was pondering whether I should tell her about the lottery money or not.

"I can't do it on my own, though. Those NA meetings aren't going to work for me, I need something more, I need to go away, I need to leave this place, but how am I supposed to do that? We don't have any money; all the rehabs have waiting lists."

"Shhhhh," I told her. "Don't get yourself worked up. If you really mean what you say, we'll work it out."

Crying, she said, "I do mean what I say. I want to live a normal life. Do you know what it's like going from place to place giving up your body and sucking dick for a high? I've done it all, Isis. For all we know I could be sick, I could be dying right now of AIDS or something. All my kids were taken from me. What kind of mother lets her kids be taken from her?"

I didn't know where all this was coming from, but I guess nearing death made you tell people things you wouldn't normally tell them. I guess nearing death made you see that life was worth living.

"How did I get here? Who found me? The last thing I remember is being in an alley taking a hit."

Oh shit, I forgot I had Trey waiting in the lobby. I sat up and told her, "I'll be right back."

"Where are you going? Please don't leave me just yet."

"Sweetie, I'll be right back, I promise. Trey Senior is the one who found you, and he's waiting in the lobby to make sure you're okay."

"Trey? Your son's father?" Her surprise was obvious.

"Yes."

"He still loves you, you know that, don't you? Whenever he sees me, he asks about you and TJ."

I didn't respond to her statement, but I did tell her that when I came back I'd have some good news to share.

"I'm so tired," she said, and closed her eyes as I walked out the hospital room into the lobby. Trey was nowhere in sight.

"Excuse me, miss," I asked the nurse behind the desk. "The man who bought Shantay Bray in, did you see him?"

"He left about five minutes ago."

I wanted to go after him, to find him, to thank him, and possibly to do something else for him, but for now my main concern was my sister.

I went back into her room to share the news about the lottery, but she was asleep and an older nurse was covering her up with a blanket.

"She's going to have a hard time the next couple of days. She's so beautiful and young. It's a shame, these drugs are taking over our children. God bless her," the nurse told me.

I knew the hard time she was talking about was getting the drugs out of her system.

"If you're going to do something like a rehab, the best time to do it would be now, as soon as possible."

I looked at the nurse and noticed she looked familiar. I read her tag. It said, *Norma Jean Hunter, LPN.*

"Listen, what I'm about to tell you must remain between us, at least for right now." Something was telling me I could trust her.

"Yes?"

Clearing my throat, I told her I was the winner of the lottery.

"What lottery?"

"The one that just came out for eleven million dollars."

"You?"

I could feel my excitement growing, speaking the words out loud. "Yes." I reached into my purse and pulled out the ticket. "I'd just found out before getting the call about my sister. I haven't told a soul."

"Well, why are you telling me?"

"Because you seem to care, because there's a sincerity in you. I need to trust someone to keep an eye on her while I run home and pack her a bag and make some phone calls about rehab and report in to the lottery commissioner. Please help me. I'll make it worth your while."

"How long do you think this will take you?"

"About a day or two."

"I might have to tell the doctor."

"Do whatever you have to. I'll be back in a couple of hours with some clothes for her."

Once in the car, I said a quick prayer. A prayer of thanks, for the money, for this opportunity, and for saving my sister, sparing her life. Not only was I going to send her to rehab, but also I wanted to do the same for Trey Senior.

Right now, all I wanted to do was get home and tell Tyrone and the kids about the millions.

When I pulled into the driveway, Tyrone was sitting in the living room. "Why haven't you called me? What happened? I was getting scared."

"Tyrone, you need to sit down."

"Sit down?"

"Yes, because what I'm about to tell you might blow your mind."

"Girl, stop acting all suspicious and shit and say what you have to say."

"You love me, right?"

"You know I do."

"You want to marry me, right?"

"Come on, Isis, what's going on?"

"Just answer my question."

"Yes, dammit, it's you who don't want to marry me."

"For richer or for poorer?" You see, on my way here, I'd done some serious thinking about life and death, about taking chances versus letting fear motivate you. I realized that I loved this man. Going on a date with another man didn't lessen that love at all. My sister almost dying made me open my eyes and heart. It made me be real and ask myself why I was holding out on Tyrone. What if something happened to him, what if he died tomorrow, would I be able to deal with it? Would I be able to handle it, and the answer was no. So I decided to come home and tell him about the money and propose all in one breath.

Now I ain't stupid or nothing, we would be signing a prenup.

"Yes, Isis. For richer or poorer. Now, would you tell me what you're talking about and what any of this has to do with your sister?"

"Nothing." And in one breath I spilled everything out. "My sister almost overdosed, and by some weird coincidence, Trey Senior was in the area and got her to the hospital just in time. I want to send her to rehab with the money I won in the lottery."

Tyrone started laughing. "Yeah, okay."

I opened my purse and pulled out the ticket. "I'm serious. I won the lottery. I'm the winner of eleven million dollars."

He looked at the ticket, looked at me, then took the ticket out of my hand and turned the television on. The numbers had been scrolling across the screen on and off all day. He read the numbers on my ticket, then the numbers on the screen.

When he looked at me again, I had this big-ass smile on my face.

"Oh shit, oh shit, oh shit." He kept repeating it over and over.

"Is that all you have to say? We're millionaires and all you can do is say 'oh shit'?"

He walked over to me, picked me up, and twirled me around.

His joy allowed me to release all the emotions I'd been holding in since I found out and went to the hospital. I started dancing, crying, jumping up and down, and saying, "We're rich, we're rich, we're rich." He was dancing right along with me. Suddenly he stopped and got this real serious look on his face.

"What? Why are you looking so serious?"

"We're not rich, you are."

Before I could ask him to marry me, the kids walked into the living room, rubbing their eyes.

"You're making too much noise," Queen said.

"Yeah," the boys said.

I ran over to them and gave them each a squeeze. "How would you guys like to go to Disney World?"

TJ and Malik started jumping up and down and chanting, "We're going to Disney World, we're going to Disney World."

"I thought we couldn't afford Disney World," Queen said.

"Well, we can now, and guess what else?" I looked over at Tyrone.

"What?" I could hear the excitement growing in Queen's voice.

I walked over to Tyrone, threw my arms around his waist, and said, "We're getting married."

8

In Need of a Break

The last five days have been the most hectic days of my life. You have no idea. I can't wait to leave for the very first vacation I've ever had. I need a break. In two days, so much has taken place.

The night I made the announcement to my family, no one could get back to sleep. We stayed up all night talking about what we would do with the money. I told the kids how much I'd won; they knew it was a lot of money but they had no idea how much our lives were about to change.

Me and Tyrone talked about us getting married in Disney.

"Don't you want a big wedding with bridesmaids and all that girly stuff?" he asked.

"No, that's not important to me. What's important is that the kids are there, and us. We don't need all that extra for-other-people stuff."

I'd yet to tell him I wanted a prenup. I wasn't sure how to broach that topic.

When we finally got to bed, I dreamed of money, of the mansion I was going to purchase, where, I didn't know, but in my dream it had a big-ass pool. As a matter of fact, it had two pools, one for adults and one for children. My bathroom was hooked up, Jacuzzi, sauna, and steam room. The kids had their own room, I was driving a white Mercedes, chilling. Tyrone said I smiled all night.

The second I woke up I called my girl Dana.

"I need to talk to you. It's important."

"Girl, I've got company right now."

I knew she was talking about that knucklehead Ricky.

"Well, get rid of him. I'm on my way over." I hung up the phone before she could say a word.

Tyrone had left for work. I told him he didn't have to work anymore. He looked at me like I was crazy.

"I love my job," he told me. Tyrone worked for the Youth Center. He ran a program for troubled boys and got paid rather well. Now, don't misunderstand me, he didn't do it for the money; he did for the love of the children, to give back to the community.

That would be one of the things I'd do with my money, give back to the community, maybe start up a program for these young girls out here.

I didn't take the kids to school, I was letting them have the day off. Hell, I might even sign them out because I would be sending them to this all-black private school on the other side of town.

They climbed in the car with me and off we went to Dana's house. "Now don't say anything about the money," I told them.

"Is it a secret?" they asked.

"I want to surprise her."

When we pulled up to Dana's house, Ricky was still there. We left him in the living room with the kids while we went into her bedroom.

"Why aren't the kids in school?"

"Because I'm taking them to Disney World."

Dana looked at me like, *Yeah right.*

"And you and Danielle are coming with me."

"What are you talking about?"

Walking to the bedroom door, I peeked out.

"What are you doing? Did you rob a bank or something?"

"Better than that, I hit the lottery."

"Stop playing, girl. You came all the way over here to play."

"I'm not playing. I'm on my way to claim the winnings now and I want you to go with me."

Dana looked at me for a good minute, and from the grin on my face realized that I was not joking. She started screaming, "Oh my God! My best friend is fucking rich!"

I had to calm her down.

"Will you come with me?"

"Ya damn skippy. How much did you win?"

Smiling even wider I said, "Eleven million."
She fainted.

When she came to, she kept looking at me, smiling. "Yo, I'm happy as hell, I feel like I won the lottery right along with you. How are you going to collect your money? One lump sum or in payments?"

"Girl, what I look like—one lump sum, that way it's taxed and over with."

Suddenly she started crying.

"What's wrong with you?"

"You're going to change. You're going to move away and I'm never going to see you again."

I couldn't even lie and say I wasn't going to change because I wanted to change, but it would be for the better. "Don't go getting all sentimental on me, not before I go to the hospital, all right."

"The hospital? What do you have to go to the hospital for?"

I realized that I hadn't told her about Shantay.

Once I finished, she gave me a big hug and said, "It's going to be okay."

The kids stayed outside the hospital room while we stepped inside. Nurse Hunter was sitting next to my sister wiping her forehead. "I was wondering when you would arrive, your sister had a hard night."

Looking at her, I said, "I could imagine."

"Oh, and I didn't let anyone know about what you told me."

Hugging her, I told her, "Thank you."

"I'll be back shortly," she told me.

Dana watched her leave, and said, "She looks like your mother."

I glanced her way again and realized that's why I had felt an instant connection with her.

Shantay surprised us both by saying, "I miss my mother."

We both looked down at her.

"I do, too." I took her hand and asked her, "Do you remember what you said to me last night?"

"Yes, and I meant every word."

"I'm going to send you to a rehab."

"How are you going to do that?"

I was so scared to tell her, because either she meant what she said and the money would push her to get clean or the money would push her more towards drugs.

"Don't you want to get your kids back?" I'd already made up my mind to get them anyway, but I needed to set this rehab situation up.

"You know I do, but you're still not telling me how you're going to send me to rehab."

Dana was all in the mix. "Girl, tell her."

"Remember those numbers you dreamed?"

"Yeah."

"Well, I played them along with my kid's ages, and guess what?"

Her eyes were brightening.

"We won, girl, we won."

Shantay started boohoo crying. That started me crying, and the next thing you know Dana was crying.

We stayed at the hospital for over two hours calling various rehabs. After leaving, Dana and I went to the lottery commissioner and turned in the ticket. Of course, they wanted to set up a press conference because a young black mother on welfare had never won before.

I didn't want to do it, because the vultures were sure to come out.

Lo and behold, one was on my porch when we pulled up.

"Daddy," Queen said, jumping out the car.

I was confused about how I felt, her acting like he was the best thing since sliced bread.

"Hey, sweetie," he said, picking her up and kissing her on the cheek while eyeing me.

I walked right by him not saying a word and he followed me in the house.

"Please don't come to my house unvited again," I told him once we were inside and Queen went to her room.

"What are you going to do, sic your boyfriend on me?"

"Why are you here?" I asked, looking him in the eyes.

"I hear you hit the big time."

Ricky must have been listening and told him.

"And?"

"Well, I want my share."

I looked at him and said, "I know you done lost your mind. Your share, what share? You are nothing to me, nothing. You're my daughter's father, nothing more. You don't get a share."

"So it's like that, you're not going to help a brother out."

"Please, Understanding, let's discuss this another time. I've got bigger concerns."

"Like getting married."

I didn't even say anything. My concerns bordered more along the lines of my sister, her kids, this press conference, and what the money would mean and how it would change my life.

"Just keep this in mind while you're being stingy—I still have those tapes we made, and the pictures, I still have those, too. I'm sure with your soon to be newfound fame, you wouldn't want those things to come out."

"I'd like for you to leave now."

"Not before I say 'bye to my daughter."

"Queen! Your dad is leaving, come say 'bye to him!"

9

A New Life

Prior to Tyrone coming over, I'd done some serious thinking. Not only was I going to talk to him about the prenup, and putting Trey Senior in rehab, but I was going to tell him about the video and pictures Understanding spoke of. Damn, in the infamous words of Biggie Small, more money, more problems. It couldn't be truer.

When Understanding and I were seeing each other, I'd agreed to let him tape us having sex. It might not seem like a big deal to some, but it was to me and still is, because not only was it me and him, but Dana, as well. Yeah, you heard right, my girl Dana, always in the mix.

No, we're not messing around now. It was a one-time, stupid thing to do. I wanted to please Understanding so bad, I was so in love with him, that I would have done anything and did almost anything for him. This probably explains why I hate him so much now.

I can recall him asking me my fantasy, and me telling him I didn't have any, that he was all I needed. The thing is, I meant that shit, too. Then he went on to tell me his, that he'd like to see me have sex with a girl. I remember being disgusted with the idea. I wasn't gay and there was no way I would do such a thing. How did I get caught up out there? Weed, wine, and the fear that he would leave me if I didn't.

I'd found out he was cheating on me and wanted him so bad that I asked Dana if she would do it with me. At first she said no, but he told her he would take us shopping. We were nineteen and never knew he was filming us or taking pictures until afterwards. He promised me he'd throw them out; obviously, he didn't.

*   *   *

The second Tyrone walked in the door, I told him we needed to talk and spilled my guts about everything—the tape, the video, and about wanting a prenup.

The tape and video he could have cared less about. "What's done is done. You were young, we've all done things we regret." Then he looked at me and said, "You do regret it, don't you?"

I guess that was his way of asking if I ever thought about it. "Of course I regret it."

I decided not to worry about Understanding and his little threat; if the man I loved wasn't concerned, why should I be? I could care less about being embarrassed. If you don't hide it, it won't hurt you.

Now, the prenup talk didn't go that well, or that easy. His big issue was trust; didn't I trust him? It didn't have anything to do with trust, I told him. If we didn't work out, I wanted to know that he wouldn't try and take me to the bank. It seemed to be happening more and more; look at Janet Jackson and Jennifer Lopez—they marry these men for love, and when it doesn't work out, the men try to take advantage. I didn't want to take a chance.

He was pissed and I expected him to be, but he also loved me and wanted to be with me, and after a little exchange of words, he agreed to sign one.

"Oh, and I want to send Trey's father to rehab," I told him just before lying down.

We went to bed without making love.

The next day arrived, and it would be the day we announced to the world my good fortune. The kids and Tyrone were coming with me. Aisha came over to my house (the perks of being a millionare) and did my hair. We also discussed me backing her financially or being a partner in her business.

When we arrived at the press conference, I became nervous. The kids were looking adorable, Tyrone was in a suit, and I had on an olive green skirt set that fit every curve on my body and to me represented money.

The press asked all the questions I expected them to. Where was I from? How did it feel to go from welfare to wealth? How did I think I would handle being rich? What did I plan on doing with the money? I must say, I handled them well. Even when one of the reporters asked if it was true that I had three children by three different men, I could have went off but I chose not to. I simply stated that it was true indeed, and that I was not ashamed; in fact, all my children were well loved.

After the press conference, we went by the hospital to pick up my sister and Trey to drop them off at the airport. They were on their way to rehab. Dana had tracked Trey Senior down and told him what I wanted to do for him. He quickly said yes. He, too, was ready to have access to his children, and he knew the only way that would happen was that he'd have to be clean.

Right after the airport, we went to the mall and shopped like it was going out of style. We would be leaving for our trip to Disney the next day, and everything from panties to shoes would be new for all of us. To go into a store and just purchase shit, not have to worry about cost, was a trip. I felt like a millionaire, full of myself. I refused to worry about anything; me, Tyrone, and the kids were going to treat this vacation like a gift because that's what it was, a gift from God, a gift and a chance.

10

The Present

When we returned from our trip, so much went down. People were coming out the woodwork claiming they were relatives, asking me to invest in this, invest in that. It was off the hook.

One of the first things Tyrone and I did was look for a house out of the 'hood. Now, don't get me wrong, I wasn't going to forget where I'd come from, but I didn't have to live there to represent, either.

I did end up giving Understanding a few thousand dollars, not to keep quiet, of course, but because he is my child's father and she would be spending time with him. He shocked the shit out of me and actually invested in a studio. Homeboy thought he was going to be the next Sean "P. Diddy" Combs.

I also purchased a small house for Dana and her daughter, and gave her a few thousand, as well. I just hoped she didn't blow it, because I did feel the need to tell her I wasn't a bank and would not be loaning and giving money every few months to anyone. Those I loved would get a lump sum and would have to do with it what they saw fit.

The biggest thing of all was, I'd located my father. As it turned out, he didn't want to leave us. My mother didn't want to be with him. When she got pregnant with me, it was because he'd come to her to try and be a family, and after a few months my mother put him out and refused to let him come see us or call us. No, it didn't excuse the fact that he didn't try harder to be a part of our lives as we were growing up, but I decided to forgive him. He'd heard about my winnings and still hadn't tried to contact me for fear I would think that was the reason he wanted to see me. That alone meant a lot.

Now, a little under six months later, Shantay just got out of rehab, we're laying up in a spa, I'm going to open Champagne and Shampoo, and Shantay is going to see her kids.

I tell you this story to say: never give up hope, never doubt, and always believe. We don't know what life holds in store for us.

One
Night . . . Six
Dreams

Dwayne S. Joseph

Acknowledgments

I'd like to first give thanks to God. Once again, you've continued to be there for me, guiding me and leading me on my predestined path. Thank you for our nightly conversations and thank you for my beautiful family.

I would next like to thank my beautiful wife, Wendy. How lucky am I to have gotten the ONE! *Tu eres mi verdad, Wendy. Mi salsa y soca queen.* Thank you for the inspiration and love you give me day in and day out. I love you. This is our dollar and a dream. Here's to our family and to our new baby girl on the way! To my *princesa*, Tatiana: One day you'll be able to read this and when you do, you'll see in words how much I love you and how truly blessed I am to have a beautiful little girl like you.

To my family: Mom, Dad, Teyana, Daren, Granny and Grandmother. I love you guys. Thank you for supporting my dream. I couldn't have asked for a better family. Vaughn—welcome. To my in-laws: You guys are the bomb! Lourdes, Russell, Grace, Ivan, Prianna, Leila. I am blessed to call you my family. Ivan . . . think we'll always have sugar in our tanks? To all of my friends: Chris, Lisa, Jessie and Jasmine, Tho, Micah and Tiffany, Gregg and Kristy, Carlos (*mi hermano*), Monte, Kenny, Lyda, Mariana, Terri, Seleina, Rob and little Robbie, Adena Walker, Lori King . . . I'm lucky to call you all my friends. To my cousins, uncles, aunts: thank you for the love and support.

Martha, you know I can't leave you out. Thank you for your belief and hard work. It is an honor to have gotten to know you!

To the readers of my first novel, *The Choices Men Make,* thank you for the e-mails and kind words. I hope you enjoy! And my next book will be out soon! To the writers who've paved the way: Thank you for inspiring me. To Portia: Thank you for everything you're doing, have done, and will continue to do for me.

To the writers on this project (my friends). Carl, I've said it before: one of the realest brothers I know. A true talent and inspiration.

Man I got your back!! Jill, my twin. Girl you're about to blow uuu-uuuuup!!! You are a gifted storyteller. That we've gotten to know each other is no accident! Angel, just like Jill, you're about to blow uuuuup!! It's been one hell of an adventure for us, hasn't it!! You are a true talent! Let's do this.

Lastly, I have to give a special thank-you to the Bookends and Beginnings Book Club of Harrisburg, Pennsylvania. You guys took a brother in and made him feel like he'd always been there! Thank you for that! I hope you enjoy!

One last note. To the New York Giants: Let's do it!

Please feel free to e-mail me: *Djoseph21044@yahoo.com* or visit www.DwayneSJoseph.com.

Dwayne S. Joseph

1

5 . . . 17 . . . 3 . . . 2 . . . 11 . . . 24.

Oh shit!

I just won the lottery. I just won the goddamn lottery worth one hundred and eighty million dollars! Hold on a minute. Let me pinch myself to make sure I'm not dreaming. Damn, that hurt. Shit, maybe my eyes are playing tricks on me. Let me double and triple-check the numbers.

Oh shit! Oh shit! Oh shit!

I am rich. Filthy. I can actually do all of the things I've day-dreamed about over and over and over. Trips from here to wherever the hell I want to go. I can buy whatever I want. I can have and do anything I want. People will do whatever I say because I'm Mr. Moneybags now. Hell, I'm not even black anymore. I'm green. And my pockets are fat. Damn, let me stop jumping up and down before that nasty crab of a neighbor beneath me, Mrs. Gershwin, starts banging on her ceiling again. I can barely walk around without her ass complaining.

Hold up a second. What the hell am I talking about? I'm Donald Trump up in this motherfucker. Fuck Mrs. Gershwin. Matter of fact, fuck anybody who had, has, or will have a problem with me. Money is power and I have both now. First things first: I'm never going back to my job again. No more sweeping, no more scraping. I'm not cleaning up a damn thing ever again. Next thing I'll do is go and find me a house somewhere. Five or six bedrooms, an in-ground pool with a diving board, three-car garage; hell, maybe I'll do like MC Hammer and put a waterfall up in there. After that I'll get rid of my hooptie and buy myself a Lincoln Navigator, a Benz, and for the icing on the cake, my dream car—a Ferrari. I'll have the finest women fighting to be at my side, because it'll be all about my Benjamins.

Ring . . . ring . . . ring . . .

I'm not even going to answer that. My days of answering my own phone are over. I'll get a butler to do that shit.

Ring . . . ring . . . ring . . . ring . . .

A butler and a chef. I'll give up cooking, too.

Beep.

Good. My answering machine got it.

"DeVante! Hey, this is Lisa. I'm here with Joe, Marcus, Nydia, and Sheila. DeVante? Are you there? Did you watch the news? Did we win? You did get the tickets, right? Call me as soon as you get this."

Click.

Shit. In my excitement I completely forgot that we all chipped in ten bucks for sixty tickets. I have to share the jackpot.

Damn.

But wait a minute. I did all the hard work. No one came with me and stood for over an hour in line to get those tickets. I have the winning tickets and no proof that they contributed anything, so it's my word against theirs. One hundred and eighty million dollars. Split six ways, that's thirty million apiece. Split one way, that's a hell of a lot more to spend.

2

He's still not answering the phone," Lisa said with a frustrated exhale. That wasn't like DeVante at all.

"Are you sure he bought those tickets and didn't just pocket our money?" Marcus asked.

Joe nodded his head. "He bought 'em. He told me he did. He's my boy. He wouldn't lie." Joe looked at everyone in the room but had doubts about what he'd said. DeVante was an alcoholic, and sixty dollars would be just enough to have a nice solo party.

Nydia shook her head vigorously. "Come on, Joe. Everyone knows he has a problem with the bottle. He could put the sixty dollars to good use."

"Not everyone!" Sheila declared. She glared at Nydia and Joe. "I did not know he was an alcoholic! If you knew about his problem, why the hell didn't someone go with him?"

Joe answered. "Look, we were all busy with our classes. DeVante was the only one who had the time to make the run."

"But he has a drinking problem!" Sheila countered. She couldn't believe they let her give her hard-earned money to an alcoholic.

"Sheila," Joe said, trying to keep his voice down, which was hard because he was starting to wonder about his friend of six years. "DeVante wouldn't spend our money like that. He has a slight problem, yes, but he's an up-front guy. Besides, he wouldn't betray the friendship I have with him."

"Then where the hell is he?" Nydia asked. "I swear, if he's drunk somewhere and didn't buy those tickets . . ."

"Hold on a second," Marcus interjected, cutting Nydia off. "While we're busy worrying about him drinking our money away, has anyone thought of the possibility of him having the winning ticket? Did it ever occur to any of you that we could all be millionaires and he's trying to keep the money for himself?"

There was silence around the room as everyone pondered the possibility. Finally, Lisa said quietly, "DeVante wouldn't do that."

"Why, Lisa?" Marcus asked. "Because you sleep with him from time to time? Oh, don't be so shocked that we know. There aren't many secrets you can hide in a school filled with nosy, talkative teenagers."

Lisa shook her head, amazed that everyone knew of her relationship with DeVante. But that was her personal business. She wasn't about to discuss it, especially not with Marcus.

"Look, Marcus," Joe said, coming to her rescue. "All Lisa's saying is that even with DeVante's problem, he is a stand-up guy. I know him. He wouldn't roll out like that."

"Well, you know what, Joe, I don't know him like that. And Nydia and Sheila aren't fucking him."

Lisa slammed her hand down on the coffee table. Marcus's last comment irked her nerves. "Before you make another ignorant-ass comment and make your boss even more angry, Marcus, why don't we just go to DeVante's place? No more jumping to conclusions. No more talking out of our mouths. Or asses, in some cases."

"Good idea," Sheila said. She was the only nonminority of the group, and she didn't want any confrontation.

"Yeah, let's go," Nydia agreed, rising with Sheila. Marcus, Joe, and Lisa stood. Lisa grabbed her car key and headed to the door.

"I'll drive." As she led the pack out of the door, she thought about all of the things she would do if they'd won the money. She said a silent prayer and hoped that she would be able to follow through on those plans if DeVante did possess the winning ticket.

Trailing behind the pack, Joe thought about his own dreams. He, too, said a couple of silent prayers. One prayer for the winning numbers, and the other praying that if it came down to it, he wouldn't have to kill his best friend. Because if they'd indeed won, he wouldn't be denied his share of the prize.

3

Ring . . . ring . . . ring . . .

They just wouldn't stop calling me. I thought about picking it up this time, but what would I say? I'd already told Joe I'd bought the tickets, and he knows I wouldn't lie to him. We met at the drug and alcohol treatment center a little over six years ago. He was hooked on heroin. My poison was coke. We came from different sides of the track, Joe from the ghetto, me from the 'burbs. Traveled different roads to end up in the same location. Joe never told me what life he was living or what brought him to that place. That's a secret he won't share with anyone. Me, I have no secrets. I was on the streets hustling and using when I got busted for drug possession. It was my second offense. I got lucky because the judge who passed down the sentence knew me from when I was a kid. In her chambers, with no one else around, she gave me an option—jail or rehab. I chose the lesser of two evils.

In the center Joe and I became fast friends because of what we had in common. Drugs had taken away everything we'd had: our possessions, our friends, and more importantly, our dignity. Together we got cleaned up and started over from the bottom. Lived in a beat-up apartment in the ghetto, and got jobs as janitors in one of the city's high schools. Six years have now gone by, and I'm still a janitor, while Joe is now the gym teacher. Getting cleaned up really opened his mind to the realization that he was meant for bigger and better things. All getting cleaned up did for me was make me realize how much I'd wasted my life and that I had no clue as to what I wanted to do.

Damn, I need a drink.

That's my new poison. I started drinking to help get rid of the urge to go back to the coke. Every time I would feel the white angel's fingertips at my neck, I'd reach for a glass and a bottle. I know I need help, but I figure it's better my liver than my brain. So I just say no with a shot of vodka, rum, gin, and juice, sometimes a little Hennessey on the rocks.

I downed two shots of Captain Black and exhaled and tried to get my thoughts right. It still wasn't too late. I could call Lisa back and let everyone know we'll never have money problems again. We're all working, so I know everyone needs the money. Sheila's white and doesn't seem to have any financial issues, but I'm sure she isn't making much as the social studies teacher. I can say the same about Nydia, although because she's a Latina, I'm sure she's making slightly less than Sheila. Marcus is copping a decent salary as the guidance counselor, but he's got four baby mamas with five mouths to feed and he's obligated to pay child support for each and every one of them. Joe's got a new family to support and one other child with an ex-girlfriend he used to get high with. Once she found out about his rise from janitor to teacher, she got cleaned up, got a job, and filed for child support.

As an underpaid assistant principal, Lisa has a baby on the way that she says is mine. No one knows about that yet. She's only two months and not showing. Lisa and I hooked up two years after I started working at the school. We're nothing official. We just satisfy an urge and keep each other from being lonely. I like Lisa. She's a beautiful and intelligent sister. She'd make a lucky man a good wife one day. Sometimes I imagine myself as that good man. But I'm just a janitor, and Lisa's too smart to be with me on the real like that. So we keep our arrangement simple. No ties. No obligations. I have no idea if this baby is really mine or if she's planning on keeping it. At thirty-five, with no education, no work experience, and no direct plan for the future, a kid is the last thing I need, but it's not my decision to make.

My phone hasn't rung in the last twenty minutes, which isn't a good sign. It can only mean one thing, which means I have about fifteen minutes to decide what I am going to do before they show up. I know they're coming because that's what I would do. Thirty million apiece is worth the visit.

4

Joe was the last to get out of Lisa's Nissan. He looked up towards DeVante's window. It had always bothered him that DeVante still lived in the apartment they'd shared. That, and the environment around it was a black hole. If you allowed it to suck you in, you would be lost for good. That's why Joe had been so determined to escape its grasp after his struggle with heroin. And because he and DeVante both knew about the difficult war against drugs, he'd wanted his best friend to rise above it all, too. But they were both men and they had to make their own decisions.

"His lights are on," Lisa said, standing beside him.

"Yeah."

"You think he's up there drunk?"

"No. The lights wouldn't be on if he were."

"You sure he bought the tickets?"

"Mmm-hmm."

Lisa touched Joe's arm. "Would he try to keep the money if we won?"

Joe looked at her and then looked back at his friend's apartment. He didn't answer as he moved away towards the door.

"What's his apartment number?" Marcus asked, scanning the building's directory.

"3G," Lisa said.

Marcus hit the button twice. Two minutes passed before he pressed it again, harder this time.

"I swear he better be up there," Nydia whispered. No one knew it, but she was extremely desperate for the money. Before her husband passed away, he'd amassed a large amount of debt, healthy enough to force them to sell their house. Her husband had owned a body shop that the Gianacotti family convinced him would be good for their business. The Gianacottis were the largest mafia family on the east side of town. And if your business was good for their business, then there was no saying no to them. They turned her husband's legitimate body shop into the city's largest chop shop, bringing in thousands of dollars a week. One night, one of her husband's coworkers accidentally caused a fire in the shop, which damaged all of the cars stored inside. It just so happened that the night before, the Gianacottis had stored a Bentley with five pounds of pure cocaine in the trunk. And when they found out about the fire, they immediately blamed Nydia's husband, claiming he set the fire as a way to "void" their contract.

Already living with a weak heart, her husband died of massive heart failure after the Gianacottis informed him that he owed them ten million dollars by beating on him. His death hadn't even been a week old before the Gianacottis approached Nydia and told her that she had a month to get them the money. Up until that point, Nydia assumed that her husband had been robbed. A debt with the Gianacottis was a debt to be paid, no matter who you were or what you knew. "He has to be up there," Nydia whispered.

Joe moved his way past Marcus. Five minutes had passed and DeVante still hadn't answered. "I know another way in."

"How?" Sheila asked.

"Like this." Joe kicked the bottom of the door twice, forcing the door to open. If there was one thing he could count on, it was the lack of quality of the doors in the ghetto. "Let's go," Joe said.

Everyone followed behind him, each wondering what the outcome would be when they reached the third floor.

5

My buzzer went off sooner than I expected, which meant that they had been calling from a cell phone. I still hadn't made up my mind. I wanted to be fair, but I kept weighing the difference between one hundred and eighty million and thirty million. The realization of what I'd heard people say finally hit me: money was a hellified drug. I was certainly feeling its effect right then and there. I knew that if Joe was with them, they'd get in without my permission. One hundred and eighty or thirty—which would it be?

The knock on my door came.

Heavy.

Insistent.

Determined.

I looked down at my feet. I had my sneakers on. Laced tightly. My coat was lying beside me. I stood up, careful not to make a sound, and went to the window in the living room, the one with the fire escape. I opened my right hand. The winning ticket was still there. I stared at it, felt it tingling in my hand. I looked at my reflection in the window's glass. It was smudged, faded, distorted. I stuffed the ticket into my wallet and shoved the wallet back into my pocket. There was more banging on the door. My hand went to the window and opened it. I guess I'd made my decision.

6

Joe and Marcus threw their shoulders into the door just as DeVante stepped onto his fire escape. They rushed into the apartment and looked quickly from left to right while the women waited behind them.

"He's not here," Joe said.

"How do you know?" Marcus asked. "We haven't even checked around yet. He could be hiding somewhere."

"Ain't no place to hide in here, man."

Lisa walked into the one-bedroom apartment. She'd never been inside of DeVante's place because he'd never let her come up. She knew that his apartment wasn't going to be pretty, but she didn't expect to see what was before her. The walls were bare and painted cream white with cracks running vertically from the floor to the water-stained ceiling. The carpeting was a worn, rust-colored mess, decorated with stains. There was little in the way of furniture. A futon, a crate with a thirteen-inch color television, a small wooden table with half-filled cartons of Chinese food. Several empty bottles of vodka, Hennessey, and rum lay scattered. Lisa cut her tour short; she didn't want or need to see any more.

"I'm still checking around," Marcus said. He moved away from them and went towards the bedroom. Joe didn't try to stop him. He just continued to stare down at the ground. Lisa followed his eyes. She saw the discarded pile of lottery tickets. She had no doubt that one would be missing. She sighed. Despite the arrangement they'd agreed upon, she had developed feelings for DeVante, and she'd thought he had feelings for her, too. She looked at Joe. It was obvious from the sullen expression on his face that DeVante's betrayal hurt him, too.

"So where is he?" Nydia asked.

"Yeah," Sheila said, still remaining by the door. She was obviously nervous. She was a long way from white suburbia.

Marcus walked back into the living room, his shoulders a little lower than before. "He's not in the back or the bathroom."

"We know," Lisa said.

"How do you . . ." Marcus started. Lisa's pointing finger cut him off. He followed her lead and saw the pile. "That lousy motherfucker. We must have won, and he's trying to keep the money for himself."

"What?" Sheila asked, stepping into the apartment for the first time.

"We won!" Nydia screamed, jumping up and down. She immediately stopped, however, as the other half of what Marcus had said hit her. "This can't be happening," she whispered.

Marcus kicked an empty bottle lying next to his foot. It shattered against the wall. "Oh, it's happening all right. That half-ass janitor is trying to steal our money. Money that I damn sure need."

"Asshole!" Nydia yelled out.

"Why?" Sheila asked softly.

"Because he's a no-good alcoholic who has no type of integrity," Marcus answered.

Lisa shook her head slowly. "There has to be another reason he's not here," she said, struggling to accept the truth. "Maybe he's on his way to my house to tell us in person. Right, Joe? Maybe he's headed over by you. DeVante wouldn't do this, right?" She grabbed Joe's arm and looked hard into his eyes. His blank expression was all the answer she needed.

"We have to find him," Nydia said. "I need that fucking money!"

"We all do, Nydia," Marcus said.

"Not like I do!"

"How the hell do you know?" Marcus said, stepping to her. At six-two, he towered over her five-three frame. "None of us are rich, and we all have bills to pay."

"Not like the bills I have," Nydia responded.

Marcus smirked. He recognized a look in her eyes that let him know that she was as desperate for the money as he was. Like DeVante was at one point, Marcus still had an addiction to cocaine. He started using it when his third baby's mama filed for child support. She had two of his five kids, whom he hardly saw. The cocaine helped to dull the stress from the holes the financial obligation tore into his pockets each payday.

One day, desperate for another high and unable to pay for it, he beat down a corner man and stole the cocaine he had on him. He knew that he had been seen, and that word would ultimately get back to one of the city's largest drug dealers, but he didn't care. He was searching for that first high he would never find to put him back on the cloud away from his reality.

That was three days ago, and he hadn't been to school or back home since then. He'd never played the lottery before, but he figured thirty million was worth it. That's why he coughed up the ten dollars for the tickets. Of course, at that time he was going to use it to retire and pay his babies' mamas off. Now he was planning on leaving the States to move to the Caribbean islands where he could avoid the child support and death wish he'd signed.

"Our bills may be different, but like I said, we all have them." Marcus stared intensely at Nydia for a pregnant second. In that brief moment, Nydia realized that their lives weren't that different. Same needs, different circumstances.

"Let's find him," Nydia said.

Marcus nodded and looked at Joe and Lisa. "You two know him better than any of us. Where the hell would your boy go? Time is of the essence here."

Joe looked away from the pile and faced Marcus. He was about to answer when he heard a soft clanging noise by the window, the window he knew had a fire escape. He moved to it just in time to see DeVante trying to sneak away.

"DeVante!"

DeVante paused for a brief second and looked up.

"DeVante, man, don't do this shit."

DeVante opened his mouth to respond, but before he could, Marcus appeared at the window beside Joe.

"You lousy-ass drunk! Don't even think about trying to keep my money!"

"Give me my money!" Nydia yelled, joining him.

DeVante looked at Joe and shook his head. He'd definitely crossed the line. "I'll see you on the flip side, Joe." He continued down the fire escape, no longer worried about the noise he would make.

"Let's go!" Marcus screamed, moving away from the window. "We can still catch him."

"I'm right behind you," Nydia said. She followed Marcus out the door to the staircase. Like a lost dog, Sheila trailed after them.

Lisa and Joe didn't move. Joe remained at the window, while Lisa stood behind him.

"They won't catch him," Joe said matter-of-factly. "DeVante knows these streets like he gave birth to them."

"So what do we do?"

Joe looked at his watch. It was 11:30. "He can't claim the money until tomorrow."

"So where does he go tonight?"

Joe didn't answer right away. He was busy thinking about the message DeVante had delivered to him. "I think I know where he's going."

"Where?"

"To a hideaway spot we used to go to together."

"How do you know?"

"He told me."

"What?"

"Look, when DeVante and I used to roll tight together, he had this way of telling me when he was going to get nice. He would always tell me that he would see me on the flip side."

"The flip side?"

"Yeah. See, the flip side for DeVante meant that he was going to temporarily lose himself and his troubles. Going to the flip side was going to get drunk, high, whatever it took. Before he made his escape, he looked at me and told he would see me there."

"What if you're wrong? What if that's not what he meant?"

"I'm not. I saw his eyes."

"But what if he changes his mind and doesn't show up where you think he'll be? That ticket is worth one hundred and eighty million dollars, Joe."

"If he's not there, we'll deal with it then. But he'll be there."

"I hope you're right."

Joe didn't say a word as he stepped past her, but he hoped he was right, too, because if DeVante wasn't where he thought he would be, then he had lost a friend.

"Are you going to tell the others where you think he'll be?"

Joe turned and faced Lisa. One hundred and eighty million dollars was out there. Split three ways was sixty million apiece. Sounded a lot better than thirty.

"No," he said bluntly.

"Wouldn't that be betraying the others?"

"They're not my friends."

"And what am I?"

Joe extended his hand. "My business partner."

Lisa accepted the offer. "And DeVante?"

"We'll see when we get there."

Lisa nodded but didn't respond. She simply thought about how powerful money's wedge could be.

7

If it wasn't for Marcus, I may have changed my mind, because it wasn't in my nature to cheat people the way I was going to. I do my dirt, but I have my morals. And even though I was halfway down the fire escape, I was having second thoughts. But when Marcus appeared and started talking his shit, calling me a lousy-ass drunk and telling me to come back with his money, my morals went south.

His money? I was the one with the ticket. I've never liked Marcus. He's always looking down on people like he's better than everyone else. Always acting like he's some kind of dignified angel floating above everyone's dirt, when the truth is he's as dirty as the rest of us. See, he doesn't know it, but I've been told all about his cocaine habit from some of the users I used to hang with. I've heard about how he snorts cocaine like a vacuum that sucks up dirt. Sure, I managed to break free from the grasp of the drug's addiction, but I know that I was one of the lucky ones. Having come from that brotherhood, I don't judge those who haven't been able to make the escape yet, and I didn't sever my ties with them completely because no one can understand what a junkie goes through like another junkie. And I am still that. I may not be snorting, but the urge is still there, always will be. I don't judge those who can't stop using because I know nothing about their demons.

Marcus isn't like that, though. He's an addict of the worst kind. The kind who says his addiction is a social one, and insists that he can stop whenever he wants to, when the truth is he'd sell his soul over and over again in search of the ultimate high. Marcus pissed me off with his attitude, and that's why I told Joe I would see him on the flip side.

I headed down the dark streets, staying invisible within the shadows. I could hear Marcus's voice leading the search party on the unusually empty streets. I could hear them yelling my name, yelling obscenities. Fuck them. I was cashing this ticket in and escaping to a place where they and my past couldn't bother me. But I couldn't escape until the morning, after I claimed the prize money. And going back to my place was not an option. So where to go? There was only one place. And it was like killing two birds with one stone.

I turned down an alley and headed to Jimmy G's. Anyone who didn't want to be found went to Jimmy G's. And I wanted to be as invisible as possible.

I discreetly made my way down the seven blocks until I reached Jimmy's. I was sure I'd already lost Marcus and his gang, but to be on the safe side, I hid in an alley across the street and took a few quick glances up and down the empty block, and only when I was positive the coast was clear, I hustled across and ducked inside. As soon as I stepped in, all activity ceased as everyone stopped doing whatever it was they were doing and looked my way. It took them seconds to size me up and see that I wasn't a threat. A junkie and alcoholic can always spot one of their own. It doesn't matter how you dress, how you look, or how high in society you climb, because we all share the same faraway gaze, the same defeated expression. The brotherhood of addiction—it is as real as any secret society.

There were a lot of new faces that I didn't recognize, but that didn't surprise me. Like the NBA, NFL, or MLB, with each new season a trade takes place and a new lost soul comes in to replace one that's been lost to free agency. Of course, in our world, free agency's either rehabilitation, jail, or death. I acknowledged with a subtle nod a few people whose contract hadn't yet expired, and then went to the bar while everyone went back to their business. Jimmy G was behind the bar, not talking, not smiling, just passing out drinks and observing. He saw me and gave me a nod. Other than Joe, Jimmy was the closest thing that I had to a friend. When I would come to get high or lose myself in spirits, he'd sit and talk to me for a few minutes. I don't know why he did because I never went out of my way to talk to him.

"I ain't seen you in here in a while," he said, approaching me.

I looked at his weathered face. With his deep wrinkles, lazy eyes, and yellowed teeth, you could almost mistake Jimmy for an addict himself. But everyone knew better, and they knew not to fuck with him. Jimmy may not be the biggest of men, but he is one of the wickedest, and he isn't afraid to die, which means that he isn't afraid of anyone. But what really makes him dangerous is that he isn't part of the brotherhood, which means that his mind is always clear, allowing him to be cognizant of everything around him. Jimmy can see things happening before they happen, like he has a sixth sense. If you step into his place with bad intentions he knows it, because he can see it in your eyes and see it in the way you move. Move wrong, look wrong, and Jimmy won't hesitate to part your broken soul from your beaten body. Jimmy caters to the lost because he has a soft spot for them. His mother was a heroin addict, his father an alcoholic. He's been a part of the dark side all his life, so he knows how bad it can be, and how strong its pull is. He caters to the lost, but he's never taken a walk on our side.

"I heard you's a janitor now and got yourself cleaned up. Heard you off that smack."

"Yeah, that's right," I said softly.

"I also heard you an alcoholic now."

I didn't respond.

Jimmy looked at me and smirked; I didn't have to respond for him to see right through me.

"So what'll it be?"

"Vodka . . . straight."

Jimmy walked away and came back a second later with a shot glass and a bottle.

"Where's your running buddy?" he asked, pouring the vodka.

"Around."

"I heard he got hisself cleaned up, too, only he ain't replace one habit with another. Heard he a gym teacher in the same high school you clean up."

"Yeah, that's about right," I said, downing the liquor and motioning for another shot.

"Joe always was smarter than you."

"Leave the bottle, Jimmy."

"You a smart guy, DeVante, and even though you don't act like it, you smarter than most people in here. You coulda been a gym teacher, too."

"Why you always trying to preach to me, Jimmy? I don't see you talking to nobody else the way you talk to me."

"Your eyes . . ."

"What about 'em?"

"They black, but they ain't as dark as most of these fools in here. Some of us are cut out for bigger and better things, only we don't know it."

"And you think I'm cut out for those things?"

Jimmy sucked his teeth. "Ain't for me to think." Saying nothing else, he walked away, leaving the bottle behind.

I grabbed hold of the bottle and poured another shot. I hated when he made me think. They say the truth hurts; well, Jimmy has never lied, and when he would tell me in his own way that I was wasting away, I would feel it. That's one of the reasons why I started getting drunk in my apartment after I started working. I didn't want to hear the truth and feel the pain. It wasn't for him to think, but he always knew.

I downed the shot, and as the liquid fire blazed a trail down my chest, I stared at my reflection in the glass behind the counter. I thought about what Jimmy had said: I could have been the teacher. Was he right? Maybe. Maybe not. I patted my pocket with the ticket in it. Guess I'll never know now. I poured another shot and then saluted myself.

Then I thought about Joe.

He was my true friend, my brother, though not by blood. Our life experiences and demons bonded us with an understanding that we would always share, and when I was on that fire escape staring up at him, I realized that I couldn't betray the friendship we had. He wouldn't have turned against me and I had to respect that. Hopefully he caught what I was saying when I told him I would see him on the flip side. If he did, would he bring the others with him? I hoped not. I hated Marcus's guts, Nydia is a pain in the ass, Sheila is a damn busybody, and Lisa . . . Lisa is special. If Joe had to bring anyone, I wouldn't be mad if it was her. I don't know if we could have been anything or not, but I do know that I could see myself happy with her. But I was going to cheat her, too. If Joe brings her, I wonder what her reaction toward me will be.

8

Joe shut off the engine to Lisa's car. They were parked behind a Dumpster in an alley around the corner from Jimmy G's. Joe insisted they park there to keep the car out of sight, just in case Marcus and the others came around. Joe's hands remained fastened around the steering wheel. Sixty million dollars was waiting for him inside of Jimmy's, or so he hoped.

He could do a lot with that money. The first thing he'd do was move his wife, Shantal, and twin sons out of the cramped two-bedroom apartment they were currently living in. Because of the drug problems he used to have, paying bills hadn't been high on his list of priorities, and as a result he'd been forced to take an apartment in a less than stellar neighborhood. He'd tried other places, but after the credit check and rental history, he was always denied occupancy. In a few hours, all of the drama he'd gone through would be over.

With his share of the money he would find a comfortable seven-bedroom home with an entertainment room for the big screen and surround-sound system he would buy. He'd give his wife the sewing room she'd always wanted; his boys would still share a room, but they'd also have a separate playroom that they could leave cluttered.

Joe wanted a basement with a bar setup; he wanted another private room for the African art he planned to collect. In the backyard he wanted an eight- to ten-foot pool, with a diving board for his back flips and belly flops, and a yard big enough to have barbecues and play football with his boys. In the front he wanted a two-car garage big enough to hold the Escalade that he would buy for himself, and the Jaguar that he would buy for his wife. He'd quit his job at the school and go after his dream to be a writer. He had a lot of pain inside that he wanted to turn into stories.

Sixty million dollars would almost give him the hassle-free life he'd only ever dreamt of having. Almost. But he still had one monkey on his back; Sharmaine Jones. His ex-something, and the mother of his other son. He and Sharmaine used to get high together back in his other life. Joe had always known that their relationship would never amount to anything. They got high and fucked, and that was about as meaningful as things got. Sharmaine wasn't supposed to be able to get pregnant; at least that's what she told Joe. And because he was probably high when she told him, he never thought twice to question her or protect himself. Her pregnancy was what finally pushed him into rehab. Their child would be his first and he didn't want him or her to have a strung-out father for a role model. Joe had suffered with a poor role model all his life with his alcoholic and abusive father.

When he made the decision to make the lifestyle change, he wanted Sharmaine to make it with him, not because he particularly cared for her, but because she was carrying his child, and he was worried about his child being affected both physically and mentally from the drug use. Unfortunately, when Sharmaine finally made the decision to give up the drugs, it was too late, and because the drugs had already done their damage, Joe's son was born with mental retardation.

His son was his pride and joy and would always hold a special place in his heart because he was his firstborn. With the sixty million he could get him the best care money could provide. But having sixty million also meant that Sharmaine would be gunning for more money in child support. And while Joe had no problem giving money for his son to enjoy, he did have a problem knowing that Sharmaine would take part in the pleasure, too. Without the sex and drugs, Joe and Sharmaine were like two rams going head to head. While he lived for his wife and all three of his boys, Sharmaine lived for Sharmaine. That was why she had sought more money after his promotion and that was why Joe knew she'd try to take him to the cleaners after she found out about his winnings. Of course the joy and pain he would experience was all dependent on DeVante being in Jimmy G's as he thought he would be.

He turned and looked at Lisa. He didn't know much about her.

He'd dealt with her on a professional level at school, but that was it. It was nothing personal against her. Joe just didn't like to get to know people. That was a habit from his drug years that stuck with him. The less you knew about people, the less chance there was for you to hurt or care when they were no longer around. She didn't know that he knew, but DeVante had told him about the pregnancy, and how she thought the baby was his. That was why Joe decided to bring her with him. Because as low-key as DeVante tried to play it, Joe knew that DeVante had feelings for her, because his body language would change whenever she was around or brought up in a conversation. Joe also knew that DeVante cared for her more than he probably even realized or was willing to admit. But DeVante wasn't the only one who was smitten. He could tell by the look and concern in Lisa's eyes when they were back in the apartment that she had deeper feelings for his friend.

Joe figured the only thing that was probably keeping them from becoming anything was DeVante's work position and financial status. Just by the way she carried herself alone, Joe could tell Lisa had high standards. The fact that she ended up with DeVante wasn't a surprise to Joe, because DeVante was a good-looking guy with a decent head on his shoulders. He'd just chosen a few bad cards from the deck he was living by. As his own wife had shown him, a good woman could do wonders for a man. Maybe the woman for DeVante was Lisa. But he was going to take her share of the money.

"Before we go in, I just want to warn you that it ain't a pretty sight in there."

Lisa raised an eyebrow and folded her arms across her chest. "I'm not a little girl, Joe."

"I understand that, but this ain't no regular run-of-the-mill dive. Shit goes on in there that your eyes probably ain't seen firsthand."

"How do you know? You don't know me or where I come from."

"You're right. I don't know you. But it don't take a genius to figure out where you're from. I can look in your eyes and figure that out."

"My eyes?"

"Yeah. They're innocent. They still have a wide-eyed quality that the people you'll see don't have. You came up in a different world, probably with good family and friends to love and care for you. The people inside Jimmy's didn't have any of that. Most of the men probably don't know who their fathers are, and the only man some of the women in there call daddy is their pimp. These people don't know anything about friendships or good times. They're all more familiar with abandonment, heartache, despair, and pain."

"So what are you, the expert?"

"Nah. I'm not an expert. I'm just a guy who's been through what all those people in there are going through. I've suffered with alcohol and I've endured through the heroin. I know what it is to want to give up because the days are too hard, too long, too bleak, and the nights are just too damned short."

"So if you're out here, why are they still in there?"

"I was lucky. I wasn't so far gone that I wasn't able to find something to live for."

"And what's that?"

"My wife and kids. They keep me going."

There was silence for a few seconds after Joe's last comment. Lisa thought about the things he'd said. He had been right; she did come up in a different world. She did have the family and friends to rely on. Her world hadn't been filled with struggle and pain. She lived what her friends often called the Cosby lifestyle. Her father was a gynecologist, her mother a lawyer.

Lisa's parents had provided nothing but the best for their only child. She went to the best schools, lived in the best neighborhoods, and wore the best clothes. They worked hard for Lisa to have the things they never had, and when she went away to law school, it was under the notion that she would give back what her parents had given her. She did that by completing the program with a 4.0 average. After passing the bar exam, Lisa was supposed to join her mother in the courtroom, but somewhere in between school and living for her parents, she woke up one morning and decided that she didn't want to take the path that her parents had lain out for her since her birth. She wanted to do something for once that didn't have her parents' seal on it. Because she'd always been fascinated by the teachers she'd had in high school, she decided that she wanted to teach. So despite her parent's protests, she went back to school and got a degree in secondary education.

She applied at inner-city schools because she wanted to work with students who didn't have things easy, and help them realize their potential to become lawyers, doctors, or business tycoons, and not just performers, sports stars, or drug dealers. In teaching, she finally achieved the feeling that money and status couldn't provide—self-satisfaction. She believed her day-to-day work was an important part of the world's struggle to become a better place. Her goal to influence at least one young student to aspire to bigger and better things was accomplished within her first two years at the school, as she became one of the most respected and well-liked teachers. The students all felt comfortable talking to her and going to her for advice on their problems and decisions for after graduation. When the school's assistant principal was fired after making advances on a female student, Lisa was asked to take over the position. No one objected.

She met DeVante two years after her promotion. Both DeVante and Joe had just completed rehab, and through their second-chance program had gotten jobs as janitors in the school. Initially, she was completely turned off by DeVante's rough appearance and his dark, don't-fuck-with-me-and-I-won't-have-to-kill-you attitude. For months they never exchanged anything more than a few idle glances. He walked through the school silently mopping and sweeping and doing whatever else was needed. They bumped into one another one night as Lisa was hurrying to get home after working late. After apologizing for the mishap and helping her to her feet, DeVante finally did something he'd wanted to do since laying his eyes on her—he introduced himself.

The two talked for an hour or so, and for the first time Lisa realized that despite his bad-boy stance and all of his toughness, DeVante was actually one of the sexiest men she'd ever laid her eyes on. His eyes were dark and mysterious, his lips full and tantalizing, his body thin but powerfully built. Even the cornrows that he wore appealed to her. There was something about his total package that brought a tingle to her spine.

DeVante had always been attracted to her. She'd seen him staring at her, his eyes often stopping to admire her Angela Bassett-like body. He never talked to her like she hoped he would. She couldn't help but wonder if her position as the assistant principal had anything to do with his reluctance to talk. Thanks to their moment of clumsiness, Lisa knew that he had no choice but to speak.

After the conversation, DeVante walked her to her car and the next day when they saw one another, their idle glances were replaced with long stares. DeVante was so much the opposite of every man she'd ever been involved with, and the more she saw him and exchanged light conversation, the more she wanted him. She finally gave in to her urge a few weeks later. She'd stayed behind to catch up on some work. But that wasn't her only reason. She'd gotten to know DeVante's schedule and she knew that he would be the only one working late that evening. When the coast was clear and she was sure no one else was in the building, Lisa sought him out.

He was in the boy's locker room, sweeping up when she entered. He looked up and saw her standing with her back to the door. Her eyes locked with his, her tongue running seductively over her lips. DeVante didn't say a word as he stepped to her and planted his lips on hers. With passionate fury the excited couple kissed. Lisa opened her mouth to welcome his tongue, which he eagerly gave her. As they kissed, Lisa wrapped her leg around his calf, while he pressed his hardened crotch against her.

"Fuck me," Lisa whispered, nibbling on his ear. "Fuck me now DeVante."

Sliding his hands under her black skirt, DeVante ripped off her thong underwear and toyed with her clit while she undid his belt and pushed down his pants and underwear with her feet. She listened to him moan as she stroked his manhood, tugging on it greedily, letting him know how much she wanted it. Lifting her in his arms, and with her back still against the door, DeVante entered her wetness slowly. Both gasped as their bodies became one. Lisa gnawed on her bottom lip to try and keep her voice down, for fear of being heard by any faculty member who could have come into the school, but it was impossible to remain quiet. The way DeVante slid in and out of her made her moist with fever, and she too began to moan, quietly at first, but with each thrusting penetration, her moans became louder until she no longer cared. She took in every inch of Devante that she could, enjoying the pleasurable pain of his girth. He palmed her behind, squeezing on it as he breathed heavily into her ear, exciting her even more. She wrapped her arms around his neck, ran her hands through his cornrows and ordered him to go deeper, faster, harder.

Lisa could tell by the way he moved that he'd been with many women before. But she was willing to bet that none were as intense as she was. She pushed herself down on him almost as hard as he thrusted upwards. Against the door, his pants sitting around his ankles, her underwear ripped and strewn to the side, DeVante and Lisa released together in a chorus of carnal love.

They continued to meet like that, coupling in the teacher's lounge, her office across her desk, the gymnasium floor, and even the auditorium, acting as though they were actors in a play of lust and eroticism. Eventually they began to meet at Lisa's home, where on her bed they took the fire to another level with toys, food and whatever else they could find. As time passed, whether she wanted to admit it or not, she was beginning to feel something other than just a sexual attraction toward DeVante. His past, which he'd explained to her, didn't bother her because she was getting to know the man underneath the rough exterior everyone else saw. He'd made mistakes and fallen into the wrong things, but like everyone else, he deserved a second chance and she wouldn't condemn him for a past she wasn't a part of. And even though he was heavily into drinking, Lisa couldn't keep herself from falling in love with him.

When she found out she was pregnant, she was both elated and frightened. She'd always wanted a child to love and care for, and raise the way her parents had raised her. But what frightened her was that her child's father was a drunk and former drug addict, which made him an addict still. When she delivered the news to him, he stayed relatively quiet. "Are you sure?" he'd asked her.

"I'm sure, DeVante. And it's yours, so don't go there with the next question."

"Wasn't going anywhere. I trust you."

"So what are we going to do?"

"What do you want to do?"

Lisa looked at him and answered honestly. "I want this baby."

"Then I guess that answers your question."

"But what about you?"

"Me?"

"Yes. This baby is yours too. I hope you don't plan on leaving this child without a father?"

"I'll take care of mine."

"Good. And what about us?"

"I don't know."

"What do you mean you don't know? I though by this point we were more than just fucking partners."

"Lisa, I don't know what we are, okay. I mean, I'm a janitor and you're an assistant principal."

"So?"

"So . . . I don't know what the hell we are or can be."

DeVante left after that, not giving her a chance to reply. That was the last conversation they'd had. She'd given her share of the lottery money to Joe, who passed on all the money to DeVante.

"I hope DeVante's in there," she said, opening her car door. "We have a lot of talking to do."

Joe nodded and stepped out of the car. He could tell by her comment and the tone of her voice that there was more than the lottery money at stake.

9

Marcus, Nydia and Sheila stepped back into DeVante's apartment. Just as Marcus had suspected, he told the others, "Joe and Lisa aren't here."

"Where could they be?" Sheila asked softly. She was getting more and more paranoid about being out on the streets. It was nearing 1 A.M.

"Where the fuck do you think they could be?" Nydia snapped, turning to face her. She was getting tired of Sheila's whining voice and timid demeanor. Thirty million dollars was at stake. "Joe and DeVante are friends and Lisa is sleeping with DeVante. Did it ever occur to you that the three of them could be trying to keep our money?"

Shelia shook her head. "No, Lisa wouldn't do that. Neither would Joe. They're good people. They wouldn't try to cheat us."

Marcus spoke out this time. "Will you wake the fuck up, you pathetic bitch! That's sixty million dollars apiece for them if they keep our share. How the hell can you say that they wouldn't try to cheat us? You don't know them. Neither do I, and neither does Nydia. We're all coworkers. That's it. Good people? Are you that damn naïve?"

"I'm not naïve, Marcus. I just don't think they would do that to us. We all need the money."

Nydia shook her head. "Will you shut the fuck up, Sheila! Just listening to you is making me sick. We all need the money. Sheila, you live in the goddamned suburbs, and you're white. What the hell do you need the money for?"

"Nydia, we all have problems, okay. Just because I'm white doesn't mean I don't need money, too."

"Shut up! Shut up! Shut up!" Nydia raged. She was one click away from attacking Sheila. "Don't say another fucking word about needing any money."

Nydia glared at Sheila, causing her to take a step back in fear. She didn't say another word as Nydia sat down. Marcus walked to the window and looked down to the fire escape where DeVante had made his escape. They'd scoured the shadows within the alleys as they searched the empty streets for him and the ticket. Thirty million dollars, that's what it was supposed to be. Now they were in danger of getting nothing.

He turned and looked at his partners. Nydia sat on the couch, her gaze fixed on Sheila. She may not have had a drug dealer out for her blood the way Marcus did, but she was as hungry for the money as he was, and she acted like it. Sheila, on the other hand, didn't seem to be nearly as desperate for the financial security the thirty million dollars could provide. Nydia had been right, Marcus surmised; Sheila was white and lived in the suburbs. She didn't need the money like they did. One hundred and eighty million split two ways was ninety million dollars apiece. Two ways, of course, was minus Sheila, DeVante, Joe, and Lisa.

"Nydia, we never checked the staircase," Marcus said. "Come with me. Sheila, you stay here in case they come in while we're gone."

Nydia looked at Marcus with raised eyebrows. "And who appointed you group leader?" she asked angrily.

"Look, just come with me. There are two staircases. I can't cover them by myself."

Nydia frowned and then stood up. "Whatever," she said. She walked toward the door and as she passed by Sheila, nudged her with her shoulder. Sheila was too afraid to complain. When they got in the hallway, Marcus motioned for Nydia to follow him. When they rounded the corner, Nydia said, "I thought you wanted to split up."

Marcus shook his head. "I just said that to get you out. I want to talk to you about something."

Nydia looked at him suspiciously. "What?"

"Listen, both you and I obviously need that money a hell of a lot more than Sheila does."

"Well, I don't know about you, but I know I need that money more than her white ass does. Damn, she makes me sick. I'm tired of hearing her voice. Talking about Joe and Lisa not being in on this with DeVante—stupid, naïve bitch. Didn't she realize that Lisa's car wasn't downstairs? How stupid can she be?"

"I saw that the car was missing, too."

"I wish we didn't have to split that money with her." Nydia folded her arms and took a peek back down the hall towards DeVante's apartment. Sheila was still in there, unwilling to move until Marcus and Nydia came back.

Marcus gave Nydia a long, hard stare. He was glad she mentioned not splitting the money with Sheila first, because now he could mention it without feeling guilty.

"Listen, we don't have to split the money with her, you know. As a matter of fact, we don't have to split the money with anyone other than you and me."

"First of all, how the hell can we not split the money with her? Second of all, we don't know where the others are, and they have the ticket."

"Look, both you and I agree that Sheila's a pain in the ass and neither one of us wants her around, so I say we get rid of her. As far as the others go, I think I have an idea as to where they could be. First things first, we get rid of Sheila."

"And how do we do that? It's not like we can just up and walk away and she won't follow, you know."

"I didn't say anything about up and walking away."

"So what do you have in mind?"

Marcus leaned closer to Nydia, so close that he could smell the Herbal Essence shampoo in her hair. Whispering softly in her ear, he said, "I say we get rid of her—permanently."

Nydia pushed him away. "Are you fucking crazy?"

"Keep your voice down!" Marcus hissed.

In a lower voice, Nydia said, "Are you out of your mind? We're not killers. Well, I don't know about you, but I'm no killer."

"Nydia, then tell me how else we can get her off of our backs. If we disappear, find the others, and get the ticket, we'll still have Sheila to deal with, because you can be sure she's going to come looking for her share. And believe me, she'll probably come with a lawyer."

"So, it's not like she can prove anything."

"It doesn't matter. The minute she brings a lawyer into the equation, our money will be held up until the matter is resolved. And you can better believe she'll fight us tooth and nail. Do you really want to go through the drama and stress of trying to prove she didn't put any money in?"

"I am not a damn killer, Marcus!"

"Don't worry, you won't be. I'll take care of Sheila. All you have to do is distract her. Confront her about something, I'll do the rest."

Nydia shook her head. She'd had enough killing with the death of her husband. She wanted no part of Marcus's plan. But she also needed that money.

"Look," Marcus said, grabbing her by her shoulders. "I don't know what you need the money for, but whatever it is, wouldn't you like to have ninety million instead of thirty? All we have to do is get rid of Sheila and get that ticket."

"And what do we do about the others? Just like Sheila, they're not going to go down without a fight, either."

"We'll take care of them if and when we have to. Ninety million dollars, Nydia. Are you with me?" Marcus locked eyes with her, refusing to let her look away.

Nydia got an image of Sheila, dead and cold. Could she live with her blood on her hands? But then she got another image of her own lifeless body, courtesy of the Gianacottis. She shook her head as tears leaked from her eyes. Marcus watched her.

"Come on, Nydia," he said evenly. "We're losing time."

Nydia shook her head again, and then bowed her head. She didn't want to die. "Okay. What do you want me to do?"

"Sheila, what the hell is your problem?" Nydia said harshly as she walked back into the apartment. She and Marcus had devised a short but simple scheme to get rid of her. Nydia would walk in and yell at her about something, while Marcus followed inside, closed the door, and did the rest. She didn't know what he was going to do, and she didn't want to know.

"What do you mean, what am I doing? You and Marcus told me to wait here in case the others came back. Isn't that what you said, Marcus?"

Marcus nodded as he stepped inside and closed and locked the door.

"Yeah, we said wait, not sit on your ass," Nydia countered. She was losing strength in her voice as nervousness and guilt began to set in.

"So what else did you expect me to do?" Sheila asked.

"I don't know. Anything. Just not sit there. Did you even look out the window to see if you spotted them anywhere?"

As Nydia did her part to keep Sheila distracted, Marcus walked around the couch slowly and found what he had been looking for. Lying on the ground was a metal paperweight of a hand holding a globe. It was a gift given to DeVante by Lisa. It was supposed to signify that the world was his to do with as he desired. Marcus picked it up discreetly, and while Nydia carried on, he walked behind Sheila.

He didn't think about anything as he lifted his arm above his head. Before his arm came down, Nydia began to scream. As she did, Sheila spun around. "What?" was all she could get out before Marcus brought the weight down on her skull, causing it to split open.

Sheila rocked back and forth as her world faded in and out. She tried to scream for help, but found herself unable to do so. She turned slowly to face Nydia, who had dropped to the ground with tears falling from her eyes. With Marcus's blow, she couldn't help but think about the blows her own husband had sustained before his death.

Sheila wobbled towards her, but before she could reach Nydia, the weight came down on her head once again. Like a tree freshly chopped at its base, Sheila fell forward. She was dead before she hit the ground.

Nydia scrambled away from Sheila's body as blood oozed from her open skull to the gray carpeting. "You killed her, you killed her, you killed her," she said over and over, tears flowing, body trembling. "You killed her, you killed her."

Marcus wiped off the paperweight with his sleeve, and then easily stepped over Sheila's lifeless body and bent down in front of Nydia. He lifted her chin with his index finger and thumb, and in a very calm but callous voice said, "No, *we* killed her. Now let's go and get our money."

10

I was on my third shot of Jack Daniels and had been watching the door when Joe and Lisa walked in. I could tell by the look on Lisa's pretty face that the décor and atmosphere of Jimmy G's was a shock to her. Granted, had I come up the way Lisa did, the place—the dim lighting; the marijuana-laced air; the prostitute giving head to a customer while her pimp watched from the side; the man, drunk and passed out in his own dribble of spit; the small group snorting cocaine openly against the far wall—might have fucked with me, too. But I didn't come up like she did, so this was nothing to me. I've been an orphan since my sixth birthday. My parents died from AIDS and drugs. My father caught AIDS from needle sharing. My mom died of an overdose shortly after his death. With nowhere to turn, I made my way to the city and became a child of the streets, and started hustling by the time I was ten. Because I had the necessary street smarts and was cool under pressure, the street dealers allowed me to become a player in their game; I became a lookout on the corners and eventually sold drugs to friends who came by and gave secret signals when the cops came around. I was arrested only once and thrown in a juvenile detention center. I found a way to escape that, though, and headed back to my street family.

I started using coke out of curiosity. I was sixteen and wanted to know what it was about the magical powder that made people give up their souls. But more importantly, I wanted to know what it was about it that made my parents give up their lives. I never planned on getting hooked, but the high I was on after snorting my first line was so damned powerful, that when I came back down to reality, I had to take another trip. I lost all respect from my "family" soon after that, and when I couldn't give up the white angel, I found my-self once again without a home. I was on the verge of death when the cops picked me up. I wanted to die, and had the judge not given me the ultimatum, I would have died and never met Joe, who is now the only family I claim.

"I'm glad you got my meaning," I said as Joe and Lisa approached me.

"Yeah, I got it," Joe said.

I looked at Joe as he watched me. I could see the subtle anger in his glare. I couldn't blame him. "I tried, but I couldn't betray our friendship," I said evenly.

"Glad to know you couldn't."

Joe sat down on the stool beside me and ordered a shot of gin for himself, and nothing for Lisa. He must have been thinking that out of the three of us to be sober, it should be her. I looked at Lisa. She watched me with angry eyes full of hurt. I had betrayed her. "I'm sorry," I started, but she put up her hand for me to be quiet.

"I know the odds are probably slim, but is there anywhere in this dump that we can go to have a private conversation?"

Jimmy looked up after her comment, and by the disgruntled look on his face, it was obvious that he'd taken offense to her description of his establishment. I reluctantly turned to him. "Jimmy . . . is the back room occupied?"

Jimmy looked from Lisa to me, and then back to Lisa again, no doubt wondering if he should indulge me. Finally, with his gaze still fixed on her, he slid a key down the bar toward me. "It is now."

When I closed and bolted the door, I turned around and was met by a heavy slap from Lisa's palm. I didn't react, although it stung like hell. Lisa tried to slap me again, but I stopped her in midswing. "You asshole," she snapped. "I can't believe you were going to cheat me, too. I could understand Marcus, Nydia, and Sheila, but me? I'm the mother of your child, damn it!"

"I'm sorry," I tried again, but like the last time, she wouldn't let me get any further.

"I know we weren't anything official, but DeVante, whether you like it or not, the sex meant something to me. I had feelings for you. It didn't matter what your job was. I didn't care about your demons of the past and I was willing to help you with the demons you have now. Yes, as much as people wouldn't agree, I was falling for your ass. I thought you cared about me, too. I didn't think I was the only one whose feelings were being flipped upside down. But it's obvious now that all I ever was to you was nothing more than just another fuck!"

Before she could say another word, I pulled her into me and planted my mouth on hers. As our lips parted, I slid my tongue to meet hers, and while we kissed I ran my hands down the curves of her back and cupped her behind, squeezing it lightly. When we parted, Lisa looked at me and said, "You were going to cheat me."

I caressed her cheek. "I know," I said.

She took my hand and placed it on her stomach. "This child *is* yours."

"I know," I said slowly.

Lisa grabbed my crotch and squeezed in a not so loving way. "I should hate you for what you were going to do to me, to our baby."

I grimaced. "I know."

She mercifully let me go and kissed me again. "No matter what happens with us, I want my share of the money."

"I know," I said, running my finger along the front of her crotch.

She took my hand and guided it down her pants for my fingers to toy with her. "I want you."

"I know," I said, playing with her wet pool.

We slowly dropped to the floor and removed our clothing. I ran my tongue from her neck to her vagina as she lay back on the linoleum tiles. With her legs spread wide for me, I dove into her pool headfirst and nibbled, licked, sucked, and pulled every inch of her. Lisa gasped as I took her to the point of explosion. After she released, she laid me back and returned the favor by doing her own version of nibbling, sucking, and biting, stopping just before I exploded. "I want you inside of me," she said, sitting atop of me.

When she eased down on me, I said, "I know."

As she rode me fiercely, making sure to punish me for my crime, I took her breasts in my hand and ran my tongue around her erect nipples. Lisa moaned while she reprimanded me, and she didn't stop until she was satisfied I had learned my lesson and exploded. Breathing heavily, she looked down at me. "We need to talk to Joe."

"I know," I said.

* * *

After dressing, we rejoined Joe at the bar. He'd already downed two shots of gin and was sipping a Heineken when we appeared from the back.

"Only because you'd have to pass me to escape did I not worry," he said.

"I told you, you don't have to worry about me betraying you," I said, sitting beside him.

He looked at me. "You had thoughts before. That's enough for me."

I didn't say anything, because he was right. As Lisa sat down beside me, Joe asked, "Are we all straight?"

Lisa nodded her head. "We straight," I said.

"Good," Joe said, smiling. "Because we got three people who we ain't straight with and by now they must be realizing that, if they haven't already."

"What are we going to do about them?" Lisa asked.

"Only one thing we can do," Joe said.

"Avoid them at all costs," I finished for him.

11

After Nydia finished throwing up in the toilet bowl, she and Marcus made a quick escape from DeVante's apartment, leaving Sheila's body on the floor to eventually be discovered. Marcus had never committed a murder before, but he now understood the thrill behind the act. It was a powerful feeling to take a life, an ultimate high. It was almost equivalent to the high he got from snorting cocaine.

After Nydia vomited, Marcus went into the bathroom, closed the door, and snorted a few lines of the cocaine he still had. The high from murder was good, but he still needed the fix. With blood on his hands and coke in his system, he was ready to find his money.

"What are we going to do now?" Nydia asked. She couldn't believe how her life had changed over a matter of a few hours as she went from being desperate for money to save her own life, to being an accomplice to murder. She couldn't get away from the sight of Sheila's head being split open, her blood spilling to the carpet, her body becoming still and lifeless. She wanted desperately to take a shower to wash off the blood that she felt all over her, yet wasn't. "Marcus, what are we going to do?"

Marcus stopped walking and turned and faced her. Since leaving DeVante's place, she'd been getting on his nerves with her sobbing, her moaning, her constant questions. "We're going to find the others."

"But how? We don't know where they went."

"I told you I think I know."

"You think you know? Marcus, we just murdered Sheila. In a few hours, someone is going to find her body, and when they do . . ."

"When they do, they will be looking for DeVante. That's why we left her body there and got rid of the evidence, remember?"

"But if the police start looking for him, that'll make it harder for us."

"Listen, Nydia, you need to stop asking me all of these damn questions. By the time anyone finds Sheila's body, we'll have found DeVante and the ticket. All we need to concern ourselves with is getting that ticket, getting our money, and then disappearing ourselves. Don't worry about the police or anyone linking us to Sheila."

"But—"

"But nothing!" Marcus yelled viciously. "No more goddamned buts! Just keep your mouth shut and follow me if you want your share of the money. Because frankly, I'm getting sick of all of your damned questions."

"What are you trying to say, Marcus? That you'll kill me, too?"

Marcus stared at Nydia, and in that brief moment, he wished he hadn't thrown the paperweight away. "Look, Nydia, I'm not talking about killing you, okay. I just want my money. Now it's after two in the morning and there's only one place I can think of where DeVante and the others could be. Can we please just go there and get what belongs to us?"

"I don't want anyone else's blood on my hands," Nydia said.

Marcus nodded. "I want that ticket, Nydia, and I want that money."

He turned around and walked away without another word, while Nydia followed with the feeling that more blood would be spilled before the sun came up. As she contemplated that real and frightening possibility, Marcus mulled over what she had asked him: would he kill her, too? He looked up toward the pale moon glowing in the black, starless sky, and looked for the man in the moon, but all he saw was his own reflection smiling sinisterly down at him. He shook his head to get the vision away and focus on the matter at hand. Jimmy G's—that's where he figured DeVante, Joe and Lisa would be. It was the only place for someone to go at this time to hide, get drugs, get drunk, or get laid. He had no doubt in his mind that he would find them there.

12

"Joe, Marcus is an addict. We need to get out of here, because I have a feeling he's gonna show up." I had been thinking about that and a bunch of other things while we sat in silence. Heavy on my mind was Lisa and her pregnancy.

Like her, I didn't know what was going to happen with us, either. I did know that I was falling in love with her and that scared me. Falling in love was something I'd tried to avoid all my life because to fall in love meant that I had to change. And I never wanted to do that. Of course, I never really had a reason to until now. I was going to be a father. My life was no longer my own to waste away. That's why I stopped downing the shots of vodka. I was going to be a father and I had to start sometime. May as well be now.

I looked at Lisa from time to time. She was lost in her own thoughts, but I'm sure we were thinking along the same lines. Joe, too, was silent. Although I never told him, I envy him. I envy the strength with which he was able to get off the drugs and not go running to another. I envy the way he turned his life around, got married, and had kids. Those were all things I never thought I would be able to do. I guess I saw myself as a drunken janitor for the rest of my life, and I never saw an end to the cycle of sweeping, scraping, cleaning, mopping, and then drowning my sorrows away until I passed out, only to begin the process again when I awoke.

But with Lisa sitting beside me, for the first time the possibility of change seemed tangible. Maybe my turn had come to be happy and free from my demons. Maybe I could turn out just like Joe. Maybe with sixty million dollars I would no longer need the alcohol and I could move on. Move on in a positive direction with my life; move on without hassles; maybe even move on with Lisa and our child.

"We need to get out of here now," I said again.

"And go where?" Joe asked.

"What about your place?" Lisa suggested.

"My place? Why not yours?"

"Because," Lisa said, "everyone's car is still by me, so we can't go there."

I agreed. "She's right, man. Your place is the best option."

"The best option? How you figure that? I got a wife and two boys at home. How's it gonna look with you and Lisa rolling in there with me past two in the morning? How do I explain that to Shantal?"

"Come on, man, Shantal knows we hang. Just tell her we were too drunk to drive home."

"Both of you?"

"Why not?"

"Come on, DeVante. You know that's not gonna fly."

"Well, make it fly, man, shit. Say whatever you have to say, just make it happen. Because I have a bad feeling that the longer we stay here, the more likely we are to run into Marcus and the others."

I looked at Joe long and hard. We needed to get out of here and crash until the morning, and his was the only place I could think of. Joe shook his head and rose from his stool. "Man, Shantal's not gonna go for this."

"Just try, Joe," I said.

"Whatever, man," Joe said, reluctantly giving in to me. "Let me at least call her and let her know we're coming. Lisa, let me borrow your phone."

Lisa reached in her purse, grabbed her phone, and handed it to him. Joe mumbled a thank-you and then walked away to make his call in private, leaving Lisa and I alone while Jimmy watched intently.

"Somethin' wrong, Jimmy?" I asked. His judgmental gaze was getting on my nerves.

Jimmy smirked. "Nothin' wrong with me. But it look like y'all got problems."

"Nah. Everything's cool on our end."

"Not what it seem like to me."

"Well, I tell you what, Jimmy, why don't you forget about what our business seems like to you and get me another drink." I gave Jimmy a hard glare. As cool as I was with him, I was in no mood for any of his comments. Jimmy obviously didn't care about what I was or wasn't in the mood for. He looked away from me and stared at Lisa.

"How 'bout you, girl? Everything cool on your end?"

Lisa nodded. "Everything's fine, and my name is not girl."

"You sure about that?" Jimmy badgered.

I'd had enough and slammed my hand down on the bar. "Listen, Jimmy, I already told you things was cool. Now why don't you stop asking questions and get my fucking drink."

Jimmy looked at me with a blank stare, making it impossible for me to read his reaction to my outburst. Things got quiet around us as everyone watched eagerly to see what Jimmy would do. No one ever spoke to him that way. After a few seconds of blank staring, Jimmy grabbed a shot glass, filled it with vodka, placed it down in front of me, and smiled. I didn't smile back.

"Listen here, you drunk-ass motherfucker," Jimmy growled quietly, leaning toward me with the smile still planted on his face. "This here is my fuckin' place of establishment. I don't like for no shit to go down here. Now when I see that somethin' may go down, I make it my business to get in whoever's business I need to get in to make sure that their shit stays on the outside.

"I don't know what the fuck you involved in, and I don't care, either. But when I hear talk about needing to get out before Marcus comes, that tells me that you involved in somethin' I don't want.

"Now I suggest you down this here drink quickly. Because after this one, there ain't gon' be no more. Ever. Swallow that drink down, and then you and your friends get the fuck out of my place and don't come back. I didn't kill you for talkin' to me that way 'cause I'm figurin' it's the alcohol that got you crazy. Talk to me that way again and ain't nobody gon' be able to identify your body after I'm through with you." Jimmy's smile never wavered the whole time, and to the average person it might have seemed like we were having a friendly conversation. No one in Jimmy's was average, though.

Never averting my gaze from his, I reached for the glass, grabbed it, and gulped down the liquid fire. As I finished, Joe appeared from the back.

"We got problems, man," he said, sitting back down beside me.

"Shantal just told me that Marcus just called my place looking for us."

"What did she say?" Lisa asked, while I stayed silent, looking at Jimmy.

"She told him the truth . . . that she had no idea where we were. I had to hang up on Shantal when she started asking questions about where I was and why Marcus was calling at this time of the night. I'm not in the mood for this drama, y'all. I'm starting to think that trying to keep this money is a bad idea. We need to re-think this, for real. DeVante, you listening to me? DeVante?"

I nodded slowly as Jimmy and I continued with our stare-down. "Let's get out of here," was my answer to Joe.

"What kind of answer is that, man?"

"It's a good one," Jimmy said, glaring at me. "A damn good one."

Joe, noticing the tension, said, "What the hell is going on here?"

"Ain't nothin' gon' on here. Just do like DeVante said and get the fuck on out."

"What the—" Joe started.

I cut him off as I got up from my stool. "Let's go, Joe. Now. Come on, Lisa." Joe looked from Jimmy to me and then shook his head and walked past me. Lisa and I followed. As we walked away, Jimmy called out, "Hey, girl!"

Lisa stopped walking, despite my attempt to keep her moving, and turned around. "I told you—" she started, until Jimmy cut her off.

"I don't give a fuck what you told me. This here's my place. If I want to call you a girl, then you a fuckin' girl. If I want to call you a bitch, then you a broke-down bitch. I make the rules and I don't follow anyone else's. Now get your narrow ass out, and if I was you, I'd get away from DeVante. He ain't about shit."

Lisa sucked her teeth and turned and looked at me. I shrugged my shoulders. What did she expect me to do? She sucked her teeth again and stormed past me. Ignoring the stares and comments from the people around me, I followed her out. As soon as the door closed behind me, Lisa said, "How could you let him talk to me like that, DeVante? He disrespected me in front of everyone."

"Just be glad that's all he did," I said.

"Excuse me?" Lisa asked, her hands planted firmly on her hips.

"Lisa, Jimmy may not be the biggest man, but he is not to be taken lightly. He has killed men for less than what went on in there. The last thing I'm gonna do is try to set him straight, especially in his place."

Joe cleared his throat. "Can someone tell me what the hell just happened in there? Jimmy ain't never had beef with us before, and everything was cool before I left to use the phone. All of a sudden, I come back and we have to leave to avoid being killed. What went down in there, man? What did you do?"

"Jimmy overheard us talking about Marcus. He didn't want any problems."

Joe nodded. "So what now?"

I shrugged my shoulders. "I don't know," I said, looking up and down the dark street. I couldn't shake the feeling that we were being watched. And I didn't mean by the crackheads in the condemned building beside Jimmy's, or the prostitute whose head kept rising periodically in the front seat of a Mercedes Benz. Although I couldn't see anyone, I was sure someone was there. Marcus and the others immediately came to mind. But if it were them, wouldn't they have confronted us right then and there?

"We need to get out of here now," Joe said.

"What about a motel?" Lisa suggested.

"I don't have the money for that," I answered.

"Same here," Joe said.

"I have money."

"Let's get going then," I said, looking up and down the streets again.

"Oh, Lisa," Joe said, reaching in his pocket. "I forgot I had to use a pay phone to make my call. Your battery is dead." He handed Lisa her phone.

"Damn," Lisa said, slipping it into her pocket. "My charger is at my house."

"We'll worry about that later," I said. "Where'd you park?"

"In the alley around the corner. We parked the car behind a Dumpster," Joe said.

"Let's move," I said, taking another glance up and down the street. Lisa noticed and asked, "What's wrong, DeVante?"

I looked at her and smirked. "I have a ticket worth one hundred and eighty million dollars in my pocket."

13

Marcus had been sitting quietly in the front seat of the Ford Expedition he'd recently acquired while he watched DeVante, Joe, and Lisa outside of Jimmy G's. Marcus used to be a regular at Jimmy's, searching for his ultimate high like everyone else. But then one night, while he was tucked away in a darkened corner, he saw DeVante walk inside and head to the bar. Too eager to drown away his misery, DeVante never noticed when the high school counselor slipped out. After finding out from Joe's wife that they weren't at Joe's house, Marcus had no doubt in his mind that his initial hunch had been right, and that DeVante and the others would be at Jimmy's.

He looked to the backseat where Nydia's body lay facedown. If she had gone along with him, she would have been able to see DeVante and the others, too. But after getting rid of Sheila and then killing the owner of the Expedition, Nydia had become uncooperative and Marcus had no choice but to kill her, too. Never in his life did he think he would be associated with the word killer. But here he was, with the blood of three people on his hands and the likelihood of more deaths to come.

He'd always thought that taking another person's life would be an impossible act for him to commit. He never understood the hows and whys of murder. But after hitting Sheila with the paperweight, Marcus understood, because he felt something he'd never experienced before—true power. Without hesitation, without remorse, just like the Grim Reaper, he'd been responsible for deciding when a person's time amongst the living was up. And that was by far the most awesome sensation he'd ever experienced. Bumps rose on his skin, his hands tingled, his heart raced, his penis became erect—all with one act. Sheila was supposed to be his only victim, but with the pull of the money growing even stronger, Marcus realized that he would do whatever it took to get the ticket. That's why he killed the teenager and took the Expedition.

He decided to steal the car while he and Nydia were walking the dark streets towards Jimmy's. With his car at Lisa's, they were losing valuable time. He needed a ride and he needed one fast. So when he saw the white teenage boy bopping his head to the sounds of Eminem while waiting for the red light to change to green, Marcus decided to help himself to the Ford.

He told Nydia of his idea, and because she was still having trouble dealing with Sheila's death, she wanted no part of the 'jacking. He didn't intend on killing the youth, but after nearly strangling Nydia to death and forcing her to distract the kid by asking for help, he was so wound up that when the teen tried to fight him off, he snapped. Lost all composure, and without hesitating, put him in a headlock and broke his neck. Because they were in a city where screams were as common as police sirens, Marcus never had to worry about anyone hearing Nydia's cries. He didn't even attempt to quiet her down. He threw the dead teen's body to the side, jumped into the idling SUV, revved the engine, slid the gear into drive, and mowed Nydia down like a piece of debris in the middle of the road. Twisted and bleeding, Nydia lay on the hard, cold concrete, gasping, fighting a losing battle to stay alive.

Charged with electricity and excitement, Marcus got out of the car, stood over Nydia, and gazed into her eyes as though she were his lover, until her last breath sighed from her lips. Marcus stared at the dead bodies for a few minutes, marveling at the high he'd once again achieved. The power, charge, and thrill of murder. He'd lost himself over and over in a futile attempt to duplicate the first-time high from the cocaine, but had never been successful. As he shoved the bodies in the car, he wished that he had turned to murder a lot sooner.

Marcus smiled and turned around in time to see DeVante and the others walking away from Jimmy's. Without turning on the lights, he turned the ignition and waited. He wanted the ticket, but he no longer wanted only his share of the money. As Lisa's car appeared from around the corner, Marcus decided that he now wanted the entire jackpot. He flexed his fingers around the steering wheel. Before the morning came, he planned on using them again to help him accomplish his goal.

14

After the front desk clerk gave us the key to our room, Joe and I went outside while Lisa took the spare key and went upstairs. I still couldn't shake the feeling that we had company. Even during the drive, I felt like we were being followed. I knew that unless I took a look around outside, I wouldn't be able to sleep in peace. Of course, as anxious and excited as I was for the next morning, I knew that sleeping was going to be the last thing I would be able to do.

"Let's split up," I said as Joe and I got outside. The crackheads and prostitutes lingering close by kept the hotel from being an average five-story resting place.

"You really think we were followed here?" Joe asked, looking around. I know he longed for the comfort and cleanliness of his bed.

I shrugged my shoulders. "I don't know. But I do know that I won't be able to relax until we check around and make sure everything's cool."

"Nydia drives a Maxima, right?"

"Yeah," I answered, nodding. "And Sheila drives a Corolla, and Marcus, a Volvo."

"What do we do if we see them here?"

I shrugged again. "We'll cross that bridge when we come to it, I guess."

"If they're here, they're going to want their share. You really willing to cut them out like this?"

I looked at Joe. "Man, at first I had some second thoughts about it because I figured we all need the money. Besides, thirty million a-piece was more than enough."

"So what changed your mind?"

I looked up to the black, starless sky. "You know, I've lived in this miserable city all my life, and I've seen everything it has to offer. And because I've had my highs and my lows, I've seen and been a part of all the good, the bad, the ugly, and everything in between the cracks and crevices that this city has to offer. But with everything I've seen, done, and come across, there is one thing I've missed out on."

I paused and took a quick glance at Joe, who looked back at me, wondering where the hell I was going with my rambling. I looked back to the sky.

"Stars, Joe. I've never seen the stars in real life. And I'm not talking about one or two. I mean the clusters that you see in the movies and on TV. The kind that the people who live in the suburbs away from the smog and confusion get to see."

"Is there some sort of significance or moral to what you're telling me?" Joe asked.

"Man, when you were staring down at me on that fire escape, I was going to change my mind. But when Marcus came out with his better-than-thou attitude and started going off on me, calling me names and shit, I said to myself right then and there, fuck it. I didn't owe Marcus, Sheila, or Nydia anything."

"What about Lisa? You were going to keep her share, too."

"I think deep down, when I let you know where I would be, I was hoping she would be with you. But you're right, I was going to keep her share."

"What are you going to do about the baby she's carrying? You two gonna stay together?"

"Joe, I love her."

"I know, man."

"She deserves better."

"As far as I can tell, she chose you."

"I know," I said.

"What was up with the stars?"

I smiled. "I'm gonna cash this ticket in, and then I'm going to take Lisa and the baby somewhere where our past is far behind us and there's nothing but stars in our sights."

"Sounds like a good plan."

"What are you going to do with your money?" I asked.

"I'm going to take Shantal and the kids and move down South

where the weather's warm and the food is right. Then, after I make sure each one of my kids is taken care of, I'm gonna go after my dream of being a writer."

"Sounds like you have a good plan, too."

"Thanks for keeping things real between us, man," Joe said sincerely.

I looked at him and nodded. "We're bonded by our demons, man."

"Ain't that the truth. I'll go to the right and check around the back," Joe said.

"Cool. I'll check the left side and the front. We'll meet back in the lobby in about ten minutes."

15

Marcus watched from his ducked-down position behind the steering wheel as Joe and DeVante split up and began their search. Marcus smiled and then quietly got out of the car, which reeked of blood and death. He pocketed the .45 he had found locked in the car's glove compartment. He'd been looking for napkins to wipe his hands with when he found it. With his teammates gone, the Ford in his possession, the gun in hand, and the ticket in sight, his night was only getting better. He never doubted that he would get the ticket or the money.

Moving away from the car, he stayed low and kept himself concealed in the shadows as he followed Joe from across the street. He kept his distance, making sure not to make a sound. He imagined himself a panther, sneaking up on its prey. Marcus waited patiently for the right moment. He would only get one shot and he didn't want to alert anyone, especially not DeVante. As Joe rounded the darkened corner and headed towards the back of the building, Marcus pulled the gun from his pocket. The time had come. He hurried across the street, turned the corner, and made his move.

"You find DeVante and that ticket yet," he said, quickly rushing behind Joe and shoving the gun into the small of his back.

Joe didn't move and barely breathed. "Marcus?" he asked cautiously after a few seconds.

"Disappointed?" Marcus asked. "Did I ruin the three-way split for you, Lisa and DeVante?"

"Marcus," Joe started, before Marcus cut him off.

"Shut the fuck up, Joe. Now let's go and find DeVante."

16

After I finished checking my side of the hotel, I went back to the lobby to wait for Joe. I finally allowed myself to relax a notch when I didn't see any signs of Marcus or the others around. I glanced at my watch. In four hours we would be able to cash in on the ticket and live like kings and queens.

I thought about Lisa up in the room, pregnant with our child. She deserved a better man than me. Someone who would love her unconditionally; someone to be her best friend, her confidant, someone that she could always depend on. I knew those were the qualities she was bringing to the table. After I cashed the ticket, I would try my hardest to match her in kind. I may not have intended to fall in love, but there was no denying that I was sprung. A smile crept onto my face as I thought about grabbing her in my arms, squeezing her tightly, and making sure she knew how I felt about her.

But my smile quickly disappeared as Joe and Marcus appeared in the lobby. Shit. Joe and I locked eyes as they approached me. Without words he let me know how bad the situation was. Marcus smiled at me. We were alone in the lobby save for the lone clerk behind the desk, who was too into his phone conversation to notice when Marcus moved the gun from behind Joe's back and pointed it at me.

"What's up, DeVante," Marcus said softly. I thought about doing something like making a quick and sudden move for the gun like the heroes did in the movies. But when Marcus pointed the gun at Joe's ribs, daring me, I quickly changed my mind. Besides, I was no hero and in real life, action was a lot slower than the action on the big screen. "I assume you have rooms since Lisa isn't here, so why don't we go up to her and the four of us have a chat."

"Nydia and Sheila . . . where are they?" I asked.

Marcus smiled. "Sheila's in your apartment lying in a pool of her own blood and Nydia didn't like the way the game you started was being played, so I kicked her off the team—permanently. Now give me the room key and let's go have that chat."

17

The ride in the elevator to the fourth floor was a quiet one, save for Marcus's whistling. He was feeling good. In less then twenty-four hours he'd discovered a side of himself that he never knew existed, and he was pleased.

Joe and DeVante kept their backs flat against the back of the elevator and watched him. They were lost in their own thoughts. Joe was thinking about his family and the possibility of never seeing them again. He wished that he had been more adamant about splitting the money the way they originally planned. Joe studied Marcus as he held the gun before him. He should never have gone along with DeVante. Thirty million should have been enough. He clenched his jaw as an image of his boys and wife flashed through his mind again. His wife, Shantal, and her full figure and sexy smile; he regretted not holding her a second longer before he left for work yesterday. And his boys: he should have hugged them tighter. Until now, he'd never thought of the possibility of them being without him. He'd planned on being there for them forever, or as close to forever as he could come. Joe fought back a tear that threatened to well and fall. For the first time in his life, his existence held importance, and unlike the other times in the past, he wanted to live.

DeVante took a quick glance at Joe, and saw the glassy sheen in his eyes. He looked back to Marcus, who smiled at him when he did. He held Marcus's gaze for a few seconds and then averted it to the .45. Marcus's index finger tapped softly on the trigger, itching to squeeze it. DeVante looked back up at him. The uppity guidance counselor was gone, and had been replaced by an insane, money-hungry individual who had visible tinges of blood on his hands and under his fingernails. DeVante thought about Lisa. He couldn't let her meet the same fate as Sheila and Nydia. He glanced at the .45 again; somehow he had to get it out of Marcus's hands.

The elevator came to a slow stop on the fourth floor and the doors slid open. Marcus flashed an evil grin and dangled the room key. "Let's go," he said.

Joe moved first, while DeVante hesitated and took a moment to give Marcus a defiant glare. Marcus smiled. "I dare you," he said, tightening his grip around the butt of the .45. DeVante wanted to make a move, but knew it wasn't the time or place. He followed behind Joe. Marcus concealed the gun in his coat pocket and walked behind them slowly. His finger was ready, and in his mind he'd already pulled the trigger. "Please do something stupid," he begged the two men.

When they got to room 414, Marcus ordered them to stop. Keeping his gun trained on them and his finger on the trigger, he slid the key into the lock and opened the door. Then he ordered them to walk in ahead of him.

"I was wondering if you two were coming back," Lisa said, just walking out of the bathroom as they walked inside. They had been gone a lot longer than they said they would, and Lisa couldn't help but wonder if they had decided to leave her behind and keep the money for themselves. Her relief was short-lived, however, as Marcus walked into the room behind them. "Marcus?" she said softly.

"In the flesh," Marcus said, revealing the gun.

"Marcus, you have a gun," Lisa said, eyeing it cautiously.

"I do, don't I?" Marcus said. "I guess that means you better do whatever the fuck I tell you to do. Now get over there on the bed. You two join her." He shoved DeVante in the back, causing him to bump into Joe. With all three people on one of the twin beds, Marcus took a moment to slip a *Do Not Disturb* sign on the doorknob outside, and then grabbed a chair from the small desk in the corner and sat down. He stared at DeVante, who returned his glare in kind. Then he looked from Joe to Lisa. The room was silent, save for a few subtle knocking noises coming from the room next to them. "I guess we're not the only ones having fun," Marcus commented. "So, what a day, huh?"

"Look, Marcus, cut the bullshit, all right," DeVante said sharply. "Let's just get down to business."

"Get down to business? What business would that be?"

"Your portion of the winnings. Forty-five million dollars."

"His portion?" Lisa asked. "What about Nydia and Sheila? Where are they, Marcus?"

Marcus scratched the back of his head with the gun and squinted his eyes. "Well, Lisa, I really couldn't stand either one of them, so I decided that they didn't deserve to have any of the money."

"What did you do to them?" Lisa asked, already knowing the answer.

In a low and unsympathetic tone, Marcus said, "What do you think?"

"My God," Lisa whispered.

"God had nothing to do with it. But anyway, enough of the small talk. Like you said, DeVante, let's get down to business. You were right . . . I did come to discuss my portion of the one hundred and eighty million dollars. One hundred and eighty million that was supposed to be split six ways until you decided to keep it all for yourself. See, at first it really bothered me that you would do such a thing. I mean, we all put money in for those tickets. We all deserved to quit the shitty school system that we slave for, and live the rest of our lives without ever having to worry about bills or never having enough to get the things we want. We were all supposed to be rich. You, Joe, Lisa, Nydia, Sheila, and myself. Thirty million dollars apiece. It should have been that simple.

"But now look at what's happened. Sheila's dead and you'll be blamed for it. Nydia is dead, lying facedown in a Ford Expedition that I had to steal to track you down. Her death is on your shoulders, and so is the teenager's whose neck I had to snap when I stole the Ford. And it doesn't even end there for you, DeVante. Because when I leave here, you will have the deaths of both Joe and Lisa to live with. All of this you caused by trying to cheat a few honest and hard-working individuals.

"Now, I admit, that sounds bad. And in a way, maybe it is. Like I said, it bothered me that you would do that to us. I mean, who the hell were you to try a thing like that? Let's face it, you're nothing but a drunk ex-druggie who cleans up the filth that teenagers leave behind. But, you see, I was upset without truly understanding what you were doing."

Marcus paused and cracked his neck. DeVante watched him

carefully. Joe sat immobile while Lisa struggled to keep her composure. Marcus continued after a chuckle.

"You want to know something, DeVante?" He paused and waited for a reply that didn't come. He stood up and walked over to the bed and stood before DeVante. He looked down at the janitor he never had any respect for, and without warning, pistol-whipped him across the face. DeVante fell to the ground while Lisa screamed. Joe made a move to help his friend who lay on the floor.

"Shut the fuck up!" Marcus screamed at Lisa. He then pointed the gun at Joe's temple. "Leave him alone. I asked him a question and I'm waiting for a reply." He looked down at DeVante. "Now, do you want to know something, DeVante?"

On the ground, with blood trickling from a gash in his cheek, DeVante said, "What, Marcus?" His head was spinning from the blow, and he had a feeling his jaw was cracked, but he refused to show how much pain he was in. He lifted himself from the ground to the bed again. "What do I want to know?"

Marcus smiled at DeVante's defiance. "I owe you a thank-you. Thanks to you, DeVante, I've come to realize that I am more of a man than I ever thought I was. I'm stronger, more determined, more confident in myself and my abilities. There is nothing that I can't handle. All of this I owe to you. But that's not all. You see, not only do I have you to thank for my personal growth, but I have to thank you for my financial growth, as well. Because after tonight, I will be one hundred and eighty million dollars richer than I was before. Now give me the ticket."

18

I kept my gaze locked on Marcus despite the lightheadedness I felt. My jaw throbbed and the pain was getting more and more intense with each passing second. I could feel the blood running down my cheek. I wanted to wipe it away, but I didn't want Marcus to see that anything was affecting me. He wanted the ticket. He wanted all of the money. The pull of the money had thrown him over the edge, and I knew that he had every intention of killing all of us if he had to. I took a slow, deep breath, and very slowly opened my mouth to speak.

"You're not getting this ticket, Marcus," I struggled to say. "You're not getting shit."

I had no idea what his next move would be, or mine for that matter, but I meant what I said. I wasn't giving him a thing. Not the ticket, not the money, not my life or Joe's and Lisa's. I had enough blood on my hands. The only other blood that was going to be spilled would have to be Marcus's. I just had no idea how that was going to happen.

Marcus shrugged his shoulders. "Your call." With nothing but a smile, he raised the gun and fired a shot, hitting Joe. Lisa screamed. I turned and looked at Joe, who was bleeding from his abdomen.

Shit!

What the hell was I going to do?

Marcus looked at Joe and then at me. "He's not dead, but he can be. Give me the ticket."

"Why are you asking?" I said, desperately trying to come up

with a plan. "Aren't you going to kill us all anyway? Why don't you do it and then take the ticket."

"I'm not going to kill you, DeVante. I want you to live with what you've caused. Now give me the goddamned ticket or else Joe's finished. And then I'll take care of Lisa."

I looked at Joe. He watched me with confused eyes, wondering what the hell I was doing. The blood continued to soak his shirt. I had no idea how bad he was hit or how long he had, but it looked bad. He needed an ambulance. By the sounds coming from the hallway, I had no doubt that the paramedics and a lot of other company that wasn't invited to the party would show up. I glanced at Lisa, who cowered on the bed against the headboard. Marcus was going to shoot Joe and then Lisa. I couldn't let that happen.

Before he could make his next move, I lurched forward and threw my shoulder into him, sending him to the ground. The .45 still remained clamped in his hand. I jumped on top of him before he could compose himself and grabbed his wrist. I slammed his hand against the floor repeatedly until he let go of the gun. Marcus kneed me in my stomach, but despite the pain and the urge to throw up, I slammed my elbow into his face. He threw a blow to the back of my head and I returned in kind with several blows to his chest and temple. We wrestled on the ground, each of us struggling to reach the gun, which lay near the door.

Lisa continued to scream, making the situation that much more confusing. I grabbed Marcus by his ears and banged his head repeatedly on the hard carpeting. Though he was fading, Marcus still had a lot of fight in him, and hit me on my nose. By the blood and the pain, I had no doubt that it was broken. With blood running down my face and trickling onto his, I continued with my assault until he was no longer moving. He was still breathing. I slowly rose from on top of him and labored over to the gun and picked it up. Lisa thankfully had quit her screaming, and was now sobbing. I looked from her to Joe. His skin was getting pale. I went to him and lifted his shirt. I was no doctor, but I knew that by the time the paramedics arrived, he would be well on his way to a better place.

"Joe," I said softly. My abdomen hurt from the knee I'd taken. "Joe, Lisa and I have to get out of here." I stared into Joe's eyes. He held my gaze and nodded.

"What do you mean we have to leave?" Lisa asked. "We can't just leave."

I looked at her. "Lisa, we have to go."

"How can you say that? We can't leave Joe here like this. We have to explain this to the police."

"Lisa, Joe is dying. And we aren't explaining shit to the cops. Once we mention everything that went down and why it went down, we will never see the ticket or the money. You know how these cops work. I'm an ex-drug addict with a record. You're no criminal, but we're both black. You really think they'll be sympathetic to our story, and when all is said and done, give us back our ticket and let us go on our merry way?"

"He . . . he's right," Joe suddenly said weakly. I turned and looked at him. Blood was bubbling from his mouth as he struggled to speak. "G-get out . . . out of here . . . now!"

I turned to Lisa. Tears flooded from her eyes. I put out my hand and nodded. Reluctantly, she took my hand and together we stood up. Before leaving, I gave Joe another long look. "I'll take care of your family. Your share is still your share."

Joe nodded.

"I'll see you on the flip side."

He nodded again and then closed his eyes.

Lisa and I left the room and managed to disappear before the cops and medics came. No one attempted to stop us as we left, which no doubt had to do with the .45 I was carrying in my hand. I had two regrets about what went down back in that hotel room. One, that I let Joe get shot. And two, that I didn't shoot Marcus when I had the chance.

19

Lisa and I passed the cops and the paramedics as they were on their way to the hotel. I was driving and made sure to keep my speed to five miles above the limit, which was not too fast and not too slow. I wasn't in the best of shape, but I'd been worse before. Most of the pain I felt was in my nose, which was swollen. Blood was still flowing from it, and I knew I would have to get medical attention eventually. But I'd do that after Lisa and I cashed in on the ticket. After the disaster at the hotel, I knew it wouldn't take long for the cops to be looking for me. Once they ID'd Joe, and called Shantal, there was little doubt that my name would come up as suspect number one or two.

That, of course, depended on whether or not they found Marcus there, which I had a bad feeling they wouldn't. I should have shot him. I had wanted to. I was just so preoccupied with wanting to check on Joe, that by the time we said our good-byes, there was no time to stop and shoot. All I could hope was that by some miracle he died after we left. If not, one of two things would happen: Either the cops would nab and question him until his face turned blue, after which he would say that I shot Joe, beat him, and took their ticket. Or he'd come to and managed to escape before anyone got there, and I'd see him again. I was hoping it would be the second option. I figured my chances were better that way. If the cops questioned him, there was no way Lisa or I would be able to cash the ticket.

Marcus had been right. What a day it had been, indeed. I went from being a down-on-his-luck, drunk ex-drug addict with no money, no car, and no real future in sight, to being a rich motherfucker who'd no doubt be wanted for questioning in one, possibly two murders. If someone had told me being rich was going to be this much fun, I might have decided to stay broke.

I stole a quick glance at Lisa. She'd barely said a word since we left the hotel. I know leaving Joe behind was a hard thing to do, but what I told her was the truth. If we were questioned, the ticket and all of our hopes and dreams would have been taken away. Joe knew it, too. After everything that went down, I'm glad I had convinced her to pay with cash and use a fake name for the room. About the only way her name could tie in to anything was if Marcus spoke to the police. As crazy as Marcus had become, I had a feeling that he'd come after the ticket himself instead of risking losing it to anyone else. I wanted to say something to Lisa, to help ease her mind. I hated her being in tears.

Damn.

Why did I ever have to try and keep that money in the first place?

Why couldn't I have just split the winnings six ways like we were supposed to? Now, just as Marcus had said, I had the blood of four people on my hands. No one would have died had I done the right thing. But it was almost as though the money were calling me. Whispering, talking, screaming, shouting—demanding that I claim it as mine. All mine. I was a murderer without actually committing an act.

I put my attention back on the road. If my instincts were correct, Marcus had gotten away before the police came and he would be chasing after us. We had a half tank of gas. It would take about forty-five minutes to reach the lottery center. I tightened my hand around the steering wheel, guiding the car down the empty streets that were slowly being illuminated by the coming dawn. After claiming our prize, I planned on taking us to the nearest airport. I'd already figured the best thing for us to do was catch a plane out of the country. Maybe go to the Caribbean somewhere, where we wouldn't have to deal with cops, questions, or stress. Now all I had to do was convince Lisa of the move.

20

Marcus had barely managed to make it to the Ford and pull off before the police and paramedics arrived. His head throbbed sharply from the damage DeVante had done, and his lip was split and swollen from being elbowed. He coughed and spit blood out of the window. He'd thought about staying and waiting for the police, but realized the stupidity of that move when he thought about the ticket and what was at stake. So before anyone arrived, he hobbled away from Joe's lifeless body and the hotel and moved as fast as his body would allow to the car.

Joe, Sheila and Nydia were out of the running. All he had to do now was catch up to DeVante and Lisa. They had about a ten-minute head start, but he had to wait until there were no more cops around before he could speed up. He drove at the speed limit while several black-and-whites sped past him. When he was certain that there wouldn't be any more company, he accelerated the car.

21

I saw the Ford coming in the rearview mirror just before it hit us. Lisa screamed as I worked to keep control of the car. Marcus rammed into us again. I hit the gas, taking the car to fifty-five on the thirty-five-mile-an-hour road. Because it was nearing seven, the lonely streets were slowly becoming littered with cars and pedestrians.

I struggled to avoid the obstacles as my mind raced, trying to figure out a way to get rid of Marcus. I needed distance. When the next side street came up, I didn't hesitate to take the turn. My hope was that because of his speed, Marcus wouldn't be able to follow. My hopes were deflated when he made the turn behind me and barreled into me again. Lisa screamed again as we scraped a parked car. I turned the wheel, determined to keep us on the road, and pressed my foot all the way down on the gas pedal.

I took another turn, my mind working, Lisa screaming. Cars blew their horns as I cut them off, pedestrians yelled and hurried to jump out of our way. I made another sudden left. Like a scene straight out of a movie, Marcus sped alongside of us, causing cars to swerve away from him. His window down, he screamed, "I'm going to kill you, DeVante, and then I'm taking my money!" Then he plowed into me.

Lisa screamed out as we barreled close to another parked car, so close that her side mirror was knocked off. Without hesitating, I pulled my wheel to the left, taking my car into Marcus's. Then, with the little bit of room I'd created, I took the next right turn, not realizing or caring that it was a one-way street. Thankfully, Marcus wasn't able to follow suit and had to jam on his brakes and turn his car around. I sped down the street as cars came toward me.

When I was halfway down the block, I looked in my rearview and saw that Marcus had just made the turn and was following. I pounded on my horn for cars to get out of my way. Horns blared back at me and obscenities were yelled. I ignored them, and when the next available left came, I took it. Then I took the next right. I weaved my way around moving cars in an effort to put more distance between my smaller Nissan and Marcus's SUV. I had about twenty seconds on him.

"He's still behind us!" Lisa yelled. "What are we going to do?"

I didn't answer her as I tightened my grip on the wheel. I took another right and found myself on a familiar straightaway. Two blocks ahead would be the entrance to the tunnel, and past the tunnel would be the main bridge into the city. I had been driving without a plan up until that point.

I sped down the road, made the necessary left to the tunnel, sped through, and headed to the bridge.

22

Marcus cursed under his breath as he pressed down on the gas pedal. DeVante had gained distance on him, but he knew where he was headed. Without regard to the other drivers or pedestrians, he followed DeVante to the tunnel and then to the bridge. DeVante had a few feet on him, but he knew that he could make that up easily. He was sure DeVante knew it, too.

As he closed the distance, he felt perspiration trickle down his forehead. He was excited; he could feel, smell, and taste the money he planned to claim. He took the car to ninety as he passed a few motorists.

"That's my money," he whispered to himself. "My money."

23

Marcus was gaining on me. By the time we reached the end of the bridge, I knew he would be upon me. I also knew that there would only be a few more hits Lisa's Nissan would be able to take. I removed the ticket from my pocket and stared at it. One hundred and eighty million dollars; one hundred and eighty million dreams to be fulfilled. I kissed the ticket, slammed on the gas, taking the car to the brink, and when I had enough room, made a sudden screeching U-turn and, without stopping, bulleted towards Marcus.

"Oh my God! DeVante, what are you doing?" Lisa screamed, pulling at my arm.

"We have to get rid of him, Lisa," I said firmly.

"Get rid of him how? By killing us? DeVante, turn around! DeVante!"

I clenched my jaws and didn't respond to her. I was in a zone. My heart raced, my adrenaline was through the roof. I didn't see anything but Marcus in the SUV. We weren't even driving on the bridge. We were alone, driving on air, two rams dueling for the sweet prize called money.

"DeVante, please," Lisa begged. "You're going to get us killed! You're going to kill the baby!"

Baby. Hearing that broke me from the trance of suicide I'd fallen into. I glanced at Lisa, glanced at her stomach. I looked back to Marcus. He was coming straight for me. That's when it dawned on me: I was playing chicken with a man who'd murdered without remorse, a man whose mind was lost.

Just before we collided, I veered off to the right, all but avoiding Marcus, save for his front end clipping my rear and sending Lisa and I fishtailing towards the side railing. Lisa's screaming grew in intensity as we spun around, while various cars swerved to avoid colliding with us. We finally came to a stop, banging against the side rail. I looked at Lisa.

"Are you okay?"

She nodded her head but didn't speak. She was in shock and I couldn't blame her. Had we been spinning any faster, I'm sure the guardrail wouldn't have kept us from falling toward the ocean. I closed my eyes slowly and whispered a thank-you for still being alive. Then it dawned on me.

Marcus.

A piercing scream suddenly erupted into the air. I looked over just in time to see Marcus still in the SUV, teetering on the edge of the bridge. The guardrail hadn't been so kind to him. He and I locked eyes for a moment. I'd won, and we both knew it. Just before the Ford fell to the waters below, Marcus smiled. I started the car and drove away before the cops arrived, thinking the trouble was behind me.

I was wrong.

I'm sitting in a jail cell.

No ticket. No money. I'm not on the beach in the Caribbean somewhere relaxing while the day goes slowly by. Nope. I'm in a cell accused of murder. Two counts, to be exact. One count for Sheila, one for Joe. I can't believe I'm in this predicament when just days ago I was a million-dollar winner.

And then all hell broke loose.

Now five people are dead. I'm in jail. And the woman who I thought I could have lived happily ever after with has betrayed me.

I've had too much time to think about how everything went down. And as I've rationalized each and every action, I've come to accept and understand that this all happened because of my greed. The only thing I don't understand is how a woman who claimed to have feelings for me could have betrayed me the way she did.

After driving away from the bridge, Lisa and I ditched her car and caught a cab. Before going to the lottery ticket claim center, we stopped at a Target, bought new shirts to change into, and tried to fix ourselves up as best as we could. My nose was still swollen, but at least the blood flow had stopped. When we finished, we caught another cab to the center. Lisa still wasn't talking, and I wasn't saying much, either. My mind was replaying the events that took place with Marcus over and over again. I still couldn't believe he had flipped the way he did. He killed four people without a care, all for the love of money.

With twenty minutes to kill before the center opened, the cab dropped us off. There was already a crowd gathered, waiting to cash in on their winnings. I prayed they weren't there for any part of my money. I looked at Lisa. Since we had a couple of minutes, I decided to talk to her about my idea for what we should do after we collected the money.

"Lisa, after we cash the ticket, I think we should head straight for the airport and catch a plane to the islands somewhere."

Lisa turned and looked at me. "The islands?"

"Yeah."

"After all that's happened, how can you even suggest that?"

"What do you mean, how can I suggest it? What other option do we have?"

"DeVante, people are dead. Innocent people have been killed for the money we're about to claim."

"And your point?"

"Don't you have a conscience? Don't you even care about those people? Or is the money that important to you?"

"Lisa, of course I care. Joe was my best friend. Do you think I'm not hurting over his death?"

Lisa crossed her arms and curled her lips. "Are you, DeVante?"

"What do you mean, am I?"

"I mean that after his death, the only thing you were concerned about was getting here to cash in on this ticket. I haven't seen you show any remorse yet."

"Damn, Lisa! We were running for our lives, remember? I didn't have time to mourn Joe yet. Why are you tripping over me like this?"

"I'm tripping because all you seem to care about is this damn money. Money that has so much blood on it, I don't know if I want to have anything to do with it anymore."

"Come on, Lisa, why are you talking this way? Now, I'm upset about what went down, but fact is fact, we didn't kill anybody."

"Didn't we? Didn't you?"

"What do you mean by that?" I asked, glaring at her.

Lisa pointed a slender finger at me. "If you would have just split the money in the first place, none of this would have happened. Nobody would be dead."

"Lisa, look, I admit, trying to keep the money was wrong, but I didn't kill anyone." Even as I said that I knew it was a lie. I continued with my denial. "Marcus is the one who really flipped and lost his fucking mind. Not me. I was the one who made sure you and Joe wouldn't be without, remember?"

"Whatever," she said, crossing her arms across her chest.

I gritted my teeth and looked at my watch. We had only ten minutes before the center opened. As far as I was concerned, it wasn't the time or the place. "Look, arguing at this point is not going to do us any good. I say we just take the money and then get out of the country. Go somewhere where we can put this all behind us."

"DeVante, I don't know if I can put this behind me. I don't know if I ever can."

"So what do you want to do, Lisa? Tell me."

"I don't know, damn it. But there's got to be something, somebody we can try and explain this situation to."

I threw my hands in the air. "Are you for real? Please tell me you're not."

"DeVante, we're accessories to murder. We—"

"We aren't accessories to anything! We didn't do shit. Marcus did!"

"Still . . . I don't know if I can just take this money like that without telling somebody what happened."

"Lisa, we're about to go and cash in a lottery ticket worth one hundred and eighty million dollars. Do you understand what that means? I have a rap sheet. You're a minority and a female. If we talk to anyone about what happened, we're screwed. We'd get no money, we'd get no new life. Hell, we'd be lucky if we didn't get jail time. I've lived the hard life and I've served my time. Lisa, I'm not going back. I'm taking that money and going somewhere where I can live in peace. I suggest you follow me with your half."

"Follow you? How do you expect me to do that? I have family and friends here."

"Send them postcards and e-mails."

"Go to hell, DeVante!" Lisa snapped, taking me by surprise. "I'm not leaving my friends and family like that. I can't do that."

"So what do you want to do, Lisa?" I asked again.

Lisa sucked her teeth and turned her back to me. I threw my

hands in the air and looked to the entrance of the center, where a wiry man with iron-gray hair was unlocking the door. When he moved away from the door, the crowd rushed inside. I turned back to Lisa and took her hand.

"Lisa, look, last night was a disaster, but it doesn't have to end on a negative note. We're rich, baby. We don't have to worry about another thing in this world. Ever. Why don't we go get our money and then talk about what we can do." I watched her intensely. I'd tried to keep my voice calm and relaxed. I looked back to the center. The crowd was getting thicker by the second. "Come on, Lisa," I begged softly.

She looked at me. I could see tears brimming in her eyes, threatening to fall.

"I don't want any more blood on my hands, DeVante," she said quietly.

I nodded. "I know. I promise there'll be no more."

Without saying another word, I took her hand.

What happened next is almost surreal.

As we walked inside, Lisa said, "I'm nervous. Let me go use the bathroom."

I nodded, and since she wasn't the only one who was excited, I decided to relieve myself, too. When I was done, I stood in front of the mirror with the ticket in my hand. I looked at myself and smiled. In a few minutes, I would be a new man, a rich man. People would no longer look down on me because I would have power. That's what money was, and I was looking forward to its benefits. I kissed the ticket, and said a prayer for Joe. I would make sure to keep the promise I'd made to him before he died.

Unfortunately, I would never get the chance, because when I left the bathroom, I was immediately rushed by two undercover police officers and placed in handcuffs.

"DeVante Smith, you have the right to remain silent. Anything you say can and will be used against you in a court of law. You have the right to an attorney. If you cannot afford one, one will be appointed to you . . ."

I didn't hear the rest of the Miranda rights being recited to me because I was too busy staring down in horror at the ground, where the ticket, which had slipped from my hand, had fallen. The officers hadn't noticed, and neither had any of the bystanders who stood around watching silently as I was escorted away.

I found out that after the police discovered Joe's body, they did what I thought they would and called Shantal, who apparently knew all about us winning the lottery. Obviously, Joe had lied about the things he'd discussed with her. After she told them how Joe and I planned to cash in on the ticket, the police visited my apartment, where they found Sheila's body, and then sent two undercover officers to the claim center to wait for me just in case I showed up. They only had my picture. Shantal never mentioned Lisa, which meant that Joe hadn't, either. I gave Lisa's name and talked about her involvement in what went down. I wasn't trying to rat her out, but she was the only person who could help clear my name. Unfortunately, Lisa seems to have disappeared.

And, oh yeah, I found out that the one-hundred-eighty-million-dollar prize was claimed.

24

You're all probably wondering what happened to me and how I could have disappeared. Well, the truth of the matter is that I am fine and I did disappear. I disappeared right after I cashed in on the lottery ticket. I was just opening the door to walk out of the bathroom when I saw the police approach DeVante. That's when I backed up and watched with the door slightly open as everything went down.

At first, I was going to come to his aid and say something in his defense, but then I saw the ticket fall from his hand. I don't know what came over me, but when I saw that, and I realized no one else had, I froze. Stayed right where I was until the police and DeVante were gone. Then I walked out and very casually went to the ticket and picked it up. I had meant what I said to DeVante about not wanting to have anything to do with the money. It was dirty money. Blood money. Up until I held that ticket, I was going to tell DeVante I wanted nothing to do with it. I went into the bathroom, not to use it, but to have a long talk with myself, and God. I wanted to do the right thing for me. Taking that money wasn't the right thing.

But when I held that ticket . . . something happened. I can't explain the feeling that came over me, but it was almost like being pricked through my fingertips with tiny needles laced with electricity. All of a sudden, whatever feelings I'd had about not wanting that money were forgotten, and for the first time I understood what strange magic had come over DeVante and Marcus and had caused them to do the things they'd done. One hundred and eighty million dollars. The ticket whispered that to me over and over, like a chant, and before I even realized what had happened, I was cashing in on the ticket, heading to the airport with my winnings, and then catching a plane to the Bahamas.

I know it seems cruel that I would betray DeVante the way I did. After all, he is my baby's father. But let's face it, without the money did I really have a future with him? And do I really want my child to grow up with him as a role model? Besides, he betrayed me first. He was going to keep that money, and had Joe never taken me with him, I would probably never have seen him again. I kept the promise DeVante made to Joe, and mailed a check for thirty million dollars to Shantal. I couldn't betray Joe, because he didn't betray me when he could have. As for the others, I never cared too much for them, so their families got nothing. As for my family, I did as DeVante had suggested. I mailed postcards and sent e-mails.

The following is a sample chapter from Carl Weber's eagerly anticipated upcoming novel, PLAYER HATERS. It will be available in February 2004 wherever hardcover books are sold.

ENJOY!

1

Wil

I pulled up in front of my house and cursed under my breath when I saw my brother Trent's black Mercedes parked in the driveway. Trent didn't show up very often, but when he did, he always found some way to piss me off. Today was no exception. I'd told that fool a thousand times to leave space for my car when he parked in my driveway. But no, his arrogant ass always had to park in the middle of the driveway so no one would scratch up his precious Mercedes Benz. I felt like taking my keys and carving my name in the black paint. Don't get me wrong. I'm not trying to hate on my brother for having a Mercedes, but his inconsiderate behavior was just one of the countless reasons Trent and I didn't get along.

When I walked into the house I got this eerie feeling that something was seriously wrong. I'd been having this uneasy feeling all day. I know it sounds crazy, but I had the same feeling right before I found out my pops had passed away. And again, right before 9/11. That's why I decided to leave work early today and come home to my family.

Now that I was home, there was no sign of them. The only sound I heard came from a radio playing upstairs. In my house, that just wasn't normal, 'cause I had a five-year-old son and a three-year-old daughter. You just don't keep kids that age quiet unless they're taking a nap. And it was way past naptime. By this time, Diane should have been in the kitchen getting ready to make dinner, the kids running around in there with her.

"Teddy! Katie! Di!" I shouted their names, but got no reply. I wondered where Trent was, too. That's when I heard this creaking sound coming from upstairs. I couldn't be positive, but it sounded like it was coming from the direction of my bedroom.

By the time I got to the top of the stairs, the creaking and the banging had gotten louder and steadier, and it was definitely coming from behind my bedroom door. There was no doubt in my mind that someone in there was gettin' their groove on. I was just praying that it wasn't with my wife. I tried to give her the benefit of the doubt. Maybe she'd gone out with the kids and my brother was taking advantage of the empty house with one of his hootchies. Why he would do it in my bedroom instead of the guest room beats the hell outta me. Except for the fact that he's nasty. He's the type who'd do it and then leave without cleaning up, letting Di and I sleep on those nasty-ass sheets.

I stood outside the door for a few seconds, listening for voices. I still wasn't sure if it was Trent in there or not. Whoever was in there was not the vocal type, 'cause except for the creaking and some heavy breathing, it was pretty silent for a while. When I finally heard a few words, I almost lost my lunch. There was no mistaking that it was my wife's voice I was hearing. Weak-kneed, I forced myself to listen to her as she coached her partner.

"Come on baby, you can do it."

Creak! Bang!

"You can do it! Just don't stop!"

Creak! Bang!

"That's it. Just a little bit more."

Creak! Bang!

"You're almost there!"

Creak! Bang!

"One more time!"

Creak! Bang!

"That's it," she shouted.

And she was right, that was it. I couldn't take it anymore. The creaking and banging had come to a halt and all I could hear was Diane's unmistakable heavy breathing. Without thinking, I walked into my son's room and snatched his Little League baseball bat out of the toy chest. Then I busted into my bedroom like I was on an episode of *Cops*.

"Ah-ha!"

"Oh my God, Wil! You scared the shit outta me!"

I turned toward Diane, who was standing at the base of her Stairmaster. She was dressed in her workout clothes, sweat dripping down her face. She hadn't been having sex at all. She'd been working out. I felt like a moron.

"Wil, what the hell is going on? And why are you carrying that baseball bat?"

I didn't answer her. I was too embarrassed.

"Goddammit, Wil Duncan! I asked you a question. Are you gonna tell me what the hell is going on?" She placed a hand on her hip.

I lowered my head and examined the bat in my hands. I didn't wanna tell her the truth, so I said something stupid to lighten the mood.

"Um, would you believe I'm thinking about trying out for the New York Yankees?"

Unfortunately, my little attempt at humor only suceeded in pissing her off.

"Hell no, I don't believe that shit. What kinda fool do I look like?" She stepped off the Stairmaster and pointed a finger at me defiantly. "Now I wanna know what's going on, Wil. And I wanna know now."

"All right," I told her. I knew the truth was probably gonna get me in more trouble than I was already in, but it wasn't worth lying. My wife could smell a lie from a mile away. So I sucked up my pride and admitted what an idiot I'd been.

"Well, when I got home I saw Tent's car parked outside. Then I heard all the noise the Stairmaster was making. And well, to be honest, Di, it sounded like someone was having sex in . . ."

She cut me off before I could finish. "And you thought . . . You thought I would do something like that in your bed, with your brother?" I could tell by her tone that she wasn't just insulted. Now she was hurt. "What kinda woman do you think I am, Wil? You know I wouldn't cheat on you. And you know I can't stand Trent."

"I know that, Di, and I'm sorry." I tried to reach out to her but she pulled away.

"Sorry ain't good enough, Wil. Not after what we've been through." Her eyes got misty. I felt like I was shrinking in front of her. "How could you? How could you think I would mess with your brother?"

"I don't know. You know how Trent is and it really sounded like you were having sex in here."

"Sounded like?" she snapped as tears began to run down her face. "You couldn't open the door and find out before you went and got a baseball bat? After everything that's happened in the past, I can't believe you're still jumping to conclusions."

I had to bite my tongue to stop from saying what I really wanted. See, Di knew a little herself about jumping to conclusions. In the past, it was her who'd nearly ended our marriage over some shit I didn't even do. She found some pictures of me in compromising positions with a few strippers, and the next thing I knew, all my shit was on the front lawn, and the police were ordering me to leave my own property. But it's not what it sounds like. I was passed out in every one of the pictures, and I didn't even know the pictures had been taken. My boys, Kyle and Allen, thought it would be a harmless joke at Allen's bachelor party to get a few shots of me and the girls with my own camera. They figured I'd get the film developed and get a kick out of their little joke. What they didn't count on was that my wife would be the one to take the film to the pharmacy and find what she thought was enough evidence to put me out on the street and threaten to move my kids down South.

The time that I was living away from my wife and kids was the worst time of my life, and it took some creative payback from my boy Jay to convince Diane that things are not always what they appear to be on film. So obviously, we'd gotten back together since that crazy misunderstanding, and for the most part we were a happy little family again. But whenever something threatened to dredge up memories of the incident, things could revert to shaky ground in a heartbeat. That's why Di was standing at the doorway, arms crossed and lip poked out, obviously still very hurt and angry.

"Oh, and for your information, Trent borrowed the van so that he could take the kids to Chuck E. Cheese. He wanted us to have a couple of hours to ourselves," she said with a smirk as she left me standing there, still clutching the bat like an idiot.

I waited about half an hour before I came downstairs and looked for Diane. I found her watching TV in the den. I was hoping that she'd cooled off a bit by now. As I explained before, Diane's been known to hold grudges. Long, drawn-out grudges. I really didn't want this to be one of those times. Especially since I was still having that eerie feeling that something bad was about to happen.

"Di," I called from the doorway.

"What?" She never looked up from the television. It was obvious she still had an attitude, but her voice was a lot more civil than it had been upstairs.

"You still mad?"

"What do you think, Wil?" She finally looked up from the TV.

"I think we should go get something to eat and put this behind us. I saw the crab man set up over on Farmers Boulevard. I was thinking about going over there and getting some crab legs. You want me to get some for you?" There was no question that Diane was upset, but if there was one thing that could help me get back in her good graces, it was crab legs. She loved them.

"You really think you're slick, don't you?" She stood up and stepped in my direction.

"Look, Di. I don't wanna fight. I made a mistake, ah'ight? I jumped to conclusions. It's not something I'm proud of, but it's not like you never jumped to conclusions." There, I'd said it. And to my surprise, she didn't go on the defensive. She just pursed her lips and looked away. I would've expected at least a little fight out of her.

"Look, Di," I pleaded, "I just wanna get past this."

"You think buying me crab legs is gonna get your ass past this?"

"No," I sighed. "I just . . ."

She picked up her purse and spoke to me without any trace of emotion.

"Let's go, Wil." She stood and looked at me as if she'd been waiting for hours. Her face didn't give any clue about her emotional state.

"You mean you're not mad?" I asked hopefully.

"Oh, I'm still mad. But I can't be mad forever. I heard you up there on that Stairmaster. It does sound like someone having sex." She spoke quickly, like she hated to be saying it at all.

I couldn't believe she was admitting I might not be such a jerk after all. After she'd left the bedroom, I'd gone to the Stairmaster and tried it out, needing to understand how I could have been so stupid. The stepping motion was a pretty steady rhythm, but being the one on it, it seemed pretty ridiculous that I could have mistaken this sound for a creaking bed. I felt even more stupid after my little experiment, but now Di was confirming that from the first floor, it really could be confusing. The corners of my mouth started to curl into a smile, but Di stopped that in a hurry.

"That still doesn't mean you're right, Wil. You should have trusted me more than that. Had a little faith."

"I know. You're right." And she was right. After our past experiences with infidelity that really wasn't infidelity, we both had to learn to be a lot more trusting.

She walked past me into the hallway and I followed. We hadn't even got halfway down the hall when the doorbell rang. I opened it, and there was Trent, holding my son Teddy, half asleep in his arms.

"What's up, playa?" He smiled at me with that devilish grin of his.

"I'm not a player. And where's my daughter?"

"Melissa's getting her outta her car seat." He handed me my son.

"Melissa? Who's Melissa?" I glanced at Diane.

"Don't look at me. When he left this house it was just him and the kids." Diane folded her arms across her chest and glared at my brother. There was no love lost between those two. "I done told you about bringing strange women around my children, Trent. Where'd you meet this one? At a gas station? Or was she hitchhiking?"

"Damn, Diane. That was cold." Trent shook his head. "But for your information, she owns her own travel agency. Matter of fact, she just got me two round-trip trickets to Hawaii for free."

"Oh, and I should trust her around my kids because she got you free airline tickets?" Diane shot Trent an evil look. "I'm not gonna tell you again. Don't be bringing strange women around my children if you expect to ever spend time with them again." She pushed me aside and headed toward the van to get our daughter.

"Yo, playa, wait until you see the body on this one," Trent whispered. "Baby got back, front. Shit, she's got the whole damn yard."

He wasn't lying, either. When Melissa walked around the van behind Diane, I had to do a double take. She was wearing a skin-tight mini dress that had to be at least one size too small and when she walked, everything important moved. She was a cute, thick sister with a cocoa face and slamming body. For a second I was almost envious of my brother.

"Trent, aren't you gonna introduce me?" Melissa shook her head playfully at his rude behavior.

"Oh, my bad." He placed his arm around her. "Wil, Diane. This is Melissa. Melissa, this is my brother Wil and my sister-in-law, Diane. Teddy and Katie's parents."

She shook Diane's hand, then I extended my hand and she took it gracefully.

"Nice to meet you, Melissa."

"It's a pleasure. You have beautiful children," she replied with a smile.

"Why thank . . ." I never finished my sentence, because that's when I got a look at her teeth for the first time. Those damn things were going in four different directions, and believe me when I tell you at least two of them were missing. I swear, with that cute face and those messed up teeth, she looked like somebody from the Addams family.

"Wil." Diane nudged me back to reality, which was a good thing, 'cause not only was I still holding the woman's hand, but I was staring at her messed-up teeth like her face was on fire.

"Yes, Di?" I finally took my eyes off Melissa and looked at my wife.

"Why don't we go in the house so that we can put these kids to bed?" That's when I realized that we were still on the front porch.

"Oh, yeah. That's a good idea. Trent, why don't you take Melissa in the den and make her a drink while Diane and I put the kids to bed?" I tried my best not to look at Melissa, 'cause if she opened her mouth I probably would have started to laugh.

"Yeah, that sounds good. But why don't me and you put the kids to bed, big brother? I got something I need to talk to you about."

I hesitated before answering. I knew he was going to curse me out about my rude behavior toward his date. Not that I didn't deserve it.

"Ah'ight." I waved. "Y'all come on in the house 'cause this boy is falling asleep in my arms."

Diane handed Katie to Trent. He followed me into the house and up the stairs. Surprisingly, he didn't say a word until after both the kids were in bed.

"Wil?" Trent tapped my shoulder as we walked toward the stairs. I sighed. I thought I was almost home free.

"Look, Trent, I know what you're gonna say. I'm sorry if I embarrassed you out there."

"Embarrass me? Embarrass me how?"

"You know. Staring at Melissa's teeth. I shouldn't have done that. I'm sorry. I'll apologize to her if you want me to."

He chuckled. "Apologize? Apologize for what? Please, Wil, that girl knows she needs a good dentist. Why you think she gave me those tickets? How you think we met?"

I had no idea what the connection could be between her crooked teeth, my brother, and some plane tickets. But knowing my brother like I did, I probably didn't want to know the answer. So I didn't ask.

"Well, if it's not about me staring at her teeth, then what did you wanna talk to me about?'

"Man, I wanted to know if you could lend me a hundred so I could take Melissa out."

"A hundred bucks? Are you crazy? You already owe me three hundred bucks."

"I know that, Wil. And I'm gonna pay you back. Shit, I wouldn't even be asking you for this if I hadn't spent my last fifty on your kids at Chuck E. Cheese's. Not that I'm complaining. You know I love them kids."

Damn, why'd he have to say that? I wasn't gonna give him shit. But now I felt bad that he spent his money on my kids. Trent was an ass, but if there was one thing I had to give him credit for, he was a good uncle. He'd do anything for my kids. I reached in my pocket and pulled out my wallet.

"I only got sixty on me."

He snatched the money outta my hand. "That'll do," he said before heading down the stairs. I looked at my empty wallet and a little voice in the back of my head whispered, *He got you again, didn't he?*

I sighed quietly to myself as I followed my brother down the stairs.

Trent and I walked into the den and found Diane sipping on a glass of wine.

"Hey, where's Melissa? She in the bathroom or something?" Trent looked around the room like she might have been hiding.

"No. She left in a cab about five minutes ago." Diane smirked.

"What?" Trent turned his head toward Diane. "Why'd she leave?"

"I don't know. Something about she had to get to her office and cancel your tickets to Hawaii."

"My tickets to Hawaii! Why? What happened?"

I wasn't sure yet what was going on, but my grinning wife obviously had some idea, and she was thoroughly enjoying herself.

Poor Trent stood there looking like his whole world was coming apart.

"Oh, yeah," Diane said a little too gleefully, "and she told me to tell you to lose her number."

"She sure told you a lot, Diane," Trent snarled at my wife. "What the hell did you tell her?"

"I ain't tell her shit. I just answered a few of her questions."

"Like what?" He was getting heated now. I didn't really think he'd get stupid up in here, but I took a few steps toward my wife just in case Trent got out of hand.

"She asked me if my husband was a dentist like his brother," Diane said with a little laugh. She looked at me, but I declined to join in on her little fun and games. Trent just shook his head. I guess he knew what the rest of the story would be. No doubt he was wishing right now he'd left the girl in the car when he dropped off the kids.

"And what did you tell her?" He had real attitude in his voice now.

"I told her that my husband ain't no damn dentist! And neither are you. What did you expect me to do, lie for you?"

Trent walked toward the door. The tension in my shoulders relaxed just a bit, knowing this latest little confrontation was almost over.

"You know what I wanna know, Diane?"

"What would that be, Trent?" She smirked at him.

"I wanna know why you always playa-hatin'." Trent didn't wait for an answer. He just walked out the door and sped away in his Mercedes.